LION AND THE BLACK

Kirk Graves

Published by Tesseract Blue
1819 Central Ave S, Ste C118
Kent, WA 98032-7501

ISBN-10: 1-7329548-2-8
ISBN-13: 978-1-7329548-2-3

www.LionAndTheBlack.com

Editor: Shai V Chea
Cover Design & Desktop Publishing: Shai V Chea

CHAPTER 1

The lingering Northwest twilight had almost completely faded into darkness when David eased his car into the parking lot of the Westside Gym. Although the lot was nearly empty, he parked the midnight-blue BMW as far from the entrance as possible, taking advantage of the fifty-yard walk to the building to stretch his leg muscles.

Just inside he paused to register at the reception desk. The receptionist caught him by surprise. She was an attractive young woman with curly blonde hair whose hazel eyes were fringed with long dark lashes.

"Hi, David, you're working out late tonight." She said with a smile.

David returned her smile politely. "This is my favorite time, after the rush. I don't have to compete for time on the machines."

"Well, you'll be happy to know that you pretty much have the place to yourself— for a few minutes anyway." The girl giggled and glanced over her shoulder at the clock on the wall behind her. "I get off in twenty minutes, so I'll see you in there."

David gave her a little nod and then turned and walked toward the men's locker room. The young woman watched him go, admiring his retreating figure. He seems like such a nice guy, and so attractive, she thought wistfully. Not for the first time she wondered what she could do to capture his attention.

David made his way to locker number G-33, twirled the dial of the combination lock, and swung open the locker door. He removed a standard-issue terry-cloth towel from a hook on the inside of the door, revealing a lone picture taped there — not a snapshot, but a photograph cut carefully from the page of a magazine. The picture featured a woman, wrapped modestly in a large bath towel, sitting on the edge of a bathtub. Evidently it was an advertisement for a hair-care product, for her long, luxuriant, coal-black hair dominated the picture. A bare shoulder revealed creamy, olive-colored skin, as did the face, which was turned away from the camera and offered only a fleeting glimpse of high cheekbones.

David hung up his street clothes and then walked naked to the dry sauna where he ran through some stretches — literally warming up. He pulled open the heavy door to find the sauna just how he liked it — empty. After dousing the coals with water, he began his routine, using the benches to help stretch his muscles. He closed his eyes, drinking in the steamy mist like a bone-dry sponge in a tropical rain, and let his mind drift. At first, he thought of nothing in particular; then slowly, steadily, inevitably, the image he could not shake appeared... that of a woman he had come to call "The Black."

As always, he did not recognize her. She stood a little taller than most women, at once slender and sexy, with skin the color of desert sand at sunset and thick ebony hair that hung down her back. Her identity however, remained a mystery for, try as he might, David could never manage to bring the woman to turn completely toward his mind's eye. Still little by little, she had begun to creep into his consciousness over the last several months, and although he knew not who she was, David had come to believe she was his destiny.

Suddenly, the door swung open and a draft of cold air wrenched David from his reverie. He peered through the amber light at the two men entering the sweltering cocoon of the sauna, at once recognizing who it was when he heard a booming voice call his name.

"David, you no-good dog! I was hoping to catch you here tonight, how ya doin?"

David smiled and removed his foot from atop the cedar boards, so he could shake hands with both men.

"Hey, Terry, Mac," David greeted them, a friendly note in his voice. "I didn't know you were here tonight."

"And I'm a hard guy to miss right?" Terry laughed, the sound deep and rich, rising up from his ample belly. He settled himself against the far wall, away from the coals. "No, I was out doing that yuppie cross-training stuff. Mac here says it's good for me." Terry jerked his head toward the slightly built man who sometimes acted as Terry's trainer. "What a waste of time! I coulda been here, pumpin' some iron."

David exchanged glances with Mac, trying to keep a straight face. He knew the value of exercising all the muscle groups, but he didn't bother to try and convince a power-lifter. He resumed his stretching, feeling no need to keep a conversation going.

Terry however, was the talkative type. "So, what have you been up to?"

"Not much, really. Work has been taking up most of my time lately."

"Yeah, tell me about it. I've been putting in sixteen-hour days at the restaurant. Whatever made me think I wanted to go into that business?" Terry complained, shaking his head.

"What is it you do again, David?" Mac asked.

"I get rid of things".

"What?"

David laughed. "I'm a liquidator. I buy things people don't need any more and then sell them to someone else." "Oh, yeah? Like what?"

"You name it— could be anything. Last week someone in Boston wanted to sell two hundred black mannequins; I found a buyer in San Diego. Yesterday I got a call to unload some women's lingerie — evidently a little too risqué for a small town down in the Bible Belt. I found a home for those in about two minutes flat."

"And you make good money doing this?"

David shrugged. "I do well, but I'm not one of the big sharks. The best thing about it is that I'm my own boss and I can set my own hours — although lately I've had to put in a lot more time than I like. But that won't last long."

Terry picked up an extra towel to wipe away the sweat pouring off his forehead. "Good, 'cause I'm going to a meet in three weeks and I want you to come as my spotter. Think you can make it?"

David had known Terry for nearly four years, and during that time he had accompanied Terry to a number of power-lifting events as his spotter. Typically, a spotter acts as a power-lifter's partner, helping him prepare mentally and physically for a meet and staying at his side at the event in case he has trouble making his lift.

But David played a more complex role for Terry. Beyond performing the more typical duties of a spotter, David also acted as Terry's bodyguard. It was not unheard of at these events for an 'accident" to happen — a barbell drops on a foot, a stray elbow flattens a nose, an illegal substance finds its way into an unattended water bottle. David's job was to make sure that nothing happened to Terry that would keep him from competing.

Terry had good reason to be careful. At forty, he was riding a five-year winning streak, not only undefeated, but the holder of several world records. More than one lifter would like to see him put out of action for a while.

"Where's the meet?" asked David.
"At the Ellensburg Rodeo. I'll be going out there the night before and I want you to come along."
David raised his eyebrows, giving Terry a shrewd look. "It'll cost you."

"Don't I know it!" Terry blared good-naturedly, still trying to stem the tide of sweat cascading down his face. "But you're the best, buddy, and you are worth it."
David rolled his eyes, amused by this not-so-subtle flattery. "All right. I'll be there."

"Hey, thanks, David. I mean it," said Terry, as he and Mac got up to leave. "I'll call you next week to set it up."

Having worked up a good sweat, David returned to his locker to dress in his workout clothes; then, grabbing his bag, he moved out into the gym where an array of exercise machines quietly awaited his attention. Although there were two or three other people in the gym, David paid them no attention. He went about his business, patiently, methodically, relentlessly going through the grueling workout routine that helped to maintain his muscular physique.

David belonged to that elite group of athletes known as world-class body builders. His involvement with the sport had begun long before it became fashionable, however. As a young boy, David had endured endless teasing, so thin and bony that he looked almost deformed — the result of living with a mother who spent what little money they had on drugs rather than food. Soon after David and his sister were moved to a foster home, his foster father enrolled him in a weight-training class for kids, and David began to blossom.

Years of working with weights did more than develop David's muscles; it built his self-esteem. He learned about discipline and determination, how to carry himself with pride, rather than arrogance. A different kind of kid might have used his newfound strength to bully his tormentors. But David, who was quiet and gentle by nature, found self-confidence in challenging himself, not others.

By the time David reached adulthood, he had developed a body that was a lean, powerful, muscular machine. More than once in his life, when he had suffered serious and debilitating injuries, he was able to make a full recovery because of the weight training he had followed so religiously over the years. About once every eighteen months, he would enter a competition, more for the challenge of getting into top form than for the thrill of winning; and out of the fifteen events he had entered in twelve years, he'd brought home seven trophies, which he proudly displayed — on a shelf in the back of his closet.

To keep in competition shape, David had developed a series of exercise regimens which he went through on a rotating basis. Tonight, he would focus on shoulders and legs. He started with the seated shoulder press, followed by a stint on the incline board, then moved on to the dumbbell shoulder raise — completing four sets of eight repetitions at each station. After each grueling set he would stretch his limbs, which flooded his muscles with blood and enhanced their development.

Next, he moved on to the squat bar, where he did twenty-five repetitious carrying 135 pounds. That was just the warmup, however. Adding enough weights to bring the load up to a backbreaking 315 pounds, he returned to his four-set, eight-repetition sequence. He finished up with leg curls and leg extensions, feeling tired but satisfied when done.

Moving to a bench where he'd left his bag, David drew out a bottle of Evian and took a long swig. As he stopped to take a breath, he looked up, his eyes unexpectedly connecting with those of the receptionist, who was madly peddling on a stationary bike across the room. She smiled self-consciously, flustered at being caught in the act of watching him. David waved at her, not because he found her intriguing, but to save her from feeling embarrassed about her obvious interest in him.

Picking up his bag, David headed back to the locker room where he peeled off his soaking clothes, then took a quick shower. After changing back into street clothes, he stopped by the juice bar for a Mango Madness smoothie and took a seat near the window. As he stared out into the moonless sky, his thoughts once again returned to The Black.

Who was she? Where was she? And how was he ever going to find her?

Although he didn't have a clue, he believed that if he kept his eyes and mind open, if he remained receptive to all possibilities, eventually she would walk into his life. And he would be ready.

CHAPTER 2

For the third time that morning, Rachel hurriedly closed and locked the front door of her cozy house behind her. As usual, she was running late, and in her haste to get out the door quickly, she had left first her purse and then her keys locked inside the house — the second problem requiring some creative breaking and entering. Now, she sprinted to her car, swearing under her breath. "Late again," she chided herself, sliding behind the wheel of her green Jaguar. "I'll just have to put my makeup on as I drive."

Every morning it seemed as though circumstances conspired to make her late for work. On Monday her cat Kido had upchucked her freshly eaten breakfast all over the carpet. Tuesday she'd had an early doctor's appointment, but the receptionist had assured her that she would have no trouble getting to work on time. That was before the screaming kid with the broken arm had been rushed in ahead of her.

This morning the culprit had been an unexpected phone call.

"Rachel." The words had been spoken softly, as though the caller were startled. "How are you?"

She had recognized the voice immediately, too shocked to reply at first. Finally finding her voice, she had stammered, "Michael. What a surprise." Hesitating, she had finally asked, "Should you be calling me?"

A low, husky, familiar chuckle had greeted her question. "To tell you the truth, I was hoping to get your answering machine. I thought you'd be at work by now."

"I don't go in until ten."

"Banker's hours. Nice."

"Not exactly," Rachel had retorted, "unless you know any bankers who work until eight. But don't evade the question. Why are you calling me and does Anita know?" Michael's sigh had been audible. "No, Anita doesn't know, nor does she want to know, would be my guess. That's why I'm calling, to tell you that Anita and I have divorced. But I was just going to leave a message. I wasn't ready to actually talk to you."

"I'm sorry to hear that," Rachel had said, genuinely sympathetic.

"Sorry that I didn't want to talk to you?" His voice had held the hint of a smile.

"No, not that." I Rachel had floundered, still unsettled by this unexpected call from the man she had almost married.

Michael had laughed at that and let her off the hook. "Just teasing you — like the old days." Then he had grown serious. "You know, it never worked for us, Anita and me. She always felt I was comparing her with you. And she was right."

Now as Rachel guided the Jag down the highway, she thought about the conversation, and about Michael. A good guy, a good catch, maybe she should give it another try?

At thirty-five, Rachel was a strikingly attractive woman, whose olive skin and black hair — the legacy of a Blackfoot Indian ancestor gave her beauty an exotic flavor. She was bright, possessed a playful, sometimes wicked sense of humor, and didn't think twice about unleashing a hot temper when it came to defending her principles. Her good looks and independent nature made her an intimidating figure to many men, and she had not yet found the man who could match her spirit.

Michael had come the closest. The owner of a lumberyard in the heart of timber country, he was wealthy and successful, with a self-confidence that comes from building one's own business from the ground up. She had admired him and genuinely cared for him but had always known in her heart that he wasn't "The One." Still, she had been jolted by his phone call this morning.

As her thoughts drifted back to their conversation, she reached into her purse and pulled out a floral makeup bag. Unzipping it, her fingers blindly searched for a tube of lipstick while she automatically checked the front, rear, and side of her car. No other cars were near her. She flipped down the driver-side visor, where a vanity mirror immediately lit up for her and, keeping one eye on the traffic and the other on her image, she slowly, carefully applied the lipstick, pursing her lips when done.

Next, her fingers felt for her hairbrush and she gave her long, straight, shiny black hair several strokes. Finally, dipping back into the small makeup bag, she pulled out the mascara, deftly unscrewed the top, and began to apply it to her already dark lashes, further accentuating her deep brown eyes. When satisfied, she flipped the visor back up and gave her full attention to her driving — just in time to see a pair of flashing red lights come up behind her.

"Great!" She groaned. "That's all I need this morning."

She pulled over quickly and retrieved the necessary documents from the glove compartment. When she turned back to the window, she found an officer there, patiently waiting for her 'to roll down the window.

"Good morning," he said pleasantly. "Your driver's license and registration, please."

Rachel handed over both, along with a card showing proof of her auto insurance.

"Did I do something wrong, officer?" she asked, almost certain that she hadn't.

The policeman didn't answer right away, making her wait and wonder, his silence feeding the growing knot in her stomach. After scanning the documents, he looked up. "Ma'am, you shouldn't be putting on makeup while you're driving."

"Oh," sighed Rachel, relieved. "I know, officer, but you see I'm late for work and I have this terrible boss — 1 mean he's really, really awful and he said if I was late

one more time I'd lose my job and I just can't let that happen because I'm a single mom supporting two kids ever since my husband ran off..."

Rachel paused for a breath, wondering what else she could say to persuade this guy to let her off.

The officer looked at her steadily. "Ma'am, I appreciate that you have a job to get to, but that does not excuse putting on your makeup in the car, that's a good way to cause an accident." Then where would your two children be?"

Rachel lowered her gaze to the hands she had folded on her lap. "You're right, officer," she said contritely. "I hadn't thought of it that way." She looked up at him and, summoning all the sincerity she could muster, she promised, "I won't do it again."

The policeman looked at her, amused. He was about forty-five and not bad looking. Rachel noticed that his hands were strong and tanned, although the yellowed fingernails on his right hand revealed that he was a smoker.

He handed the papers back to Rachel, but as she reached for them, he maintained his grasp. She lifted her eyes to his, questioning.

"I'm going to hold you to that promise," he said, "and I'm on this highway every day, so I'll be watching." His speech completed, he released his grip.

"I hear you," Rachel replied. And then she gave him a big smile, her brilliant white teeth shown off by the perfectly painted lips. "Thank you!"

By the time Rachel pulled into her reserved parking spot at The Evergreen News, it was ten-thirty. She was so late this morning she didn't pause as she usually did to admire the ancient and stately edifice, with its ornate molding, well-seasoned brick and lush green cover of climbing ivy. Instead, she pushed hurriedly through the lead-glass front doors and dashed up the stairs to her office, where her secretary, Ellen, was on the phone, trying to placate an irate caller. Seeing the forest of yellow post-it notes surrounding Ellen — sticking to her monitor, her calculator, her telephone — Rachel had a pretty good idea what kind of a day it was going to be. Motioning to Ellen that she'd be right back, Rachel grabbed her coffee cup and headed down the hall to the break room.

Miko, the receptionist in the front office, was just brewing a fresh pot of coffee. "Hi, Rachel," she said, her words softened pleasantly by a slight Asian accent. "You just getting here?"

"Don't start," Rachel warned her, but she rolled her eyes with such exaggeration that Miko laughed.

"Bad morning?"

"Got pulled over on the way here," Rachel admitted.

"For putting my makeup on in the car! Can you believe it?'

"Yes, I can believe it," replied Miko, who didn't care much for policemen, having been unhappily married to one for several years. "Did you get a ticket?"

"No, I told him how I'd lose my job if I was late and then my fatherless children would starve."

"You don't have any kids."

"Luckily, he didn't know that. Anyway, it worked, but I had to promise never to do it again. Now I have to get up ten minutes earlier every morning." She filled her cup with the steaming coffee and added some powdered creamer. "Mmmmm, nice and strong. Just what I need to face the mess waiting for me back in 'the hole.' See you later."

Returning to her office, Rachel stopped to pick up her messages, then continued to what she lovingly called "the hole" where she took a seat behind her desk. As director of personnel, she rated an office with windows and a secretary of her own. The space was small and the furniture cheap, but Ellen was a jewel. When she had finished her phone call, the secretary joined Rachel in her office.

"Whew! What a morning! Is it time to go home yet?" she asked plaintively.

Rachel gave her a grimace. "I wish. I just bet today's going to be a bear. You'd better get another shot of caffeine," she suggested, raising her cup in mock salute. "Okay, what have you got?"

Ellen ran down the many crises, imagined and real, that had been routed to their department for remedy. Rachel took notes and together they plotted their strategy for the day.

Like every other newspaper, The Evergreen News suffered from a high rate of employee turnover, especially in the lower ranks of bundle-drop drivers and newspaper carriers. Although the district managers were the ones directly responsible for keeping these positions filled, invariably Rachel had to pick up the slack when one of the managers was out sick or on vacation or, as was becoming more frequent, let go and not replaced.

The Evergreen News was a small newspaper, filled with local news and advertising and delivered to 50,000 subscribers six days a week. But on Wednesday and Saturday, circulation exploded to include an additional 235,000 homes, thanks to the subsidy of area retailers whose advertisements were stuffed in the paper. This additional burden on the drivers and carriers invariably caused personnel problems, a sore point between Rachel and the tight-fisted management.

Typically, drivers and carriers signed on thinking their job would be an easy way to make money. Too late they found out that it was tedious work, especially on those two high-circulation days, often workers stayed on just long enough to collect their first paycheck and were never seen again.

Today was one of those days where Rachel had to scramble to fill all the open down-line jobs. By 3 P.M., when the drivers were supposed to be in the loading bay picking up their bundles, she had succeeded in filling every spot. She glanced at her watch and decided to wander down to the loading dock. Since some of her new hires would be struggling through their first afternoon of work, she could help direct traffic.

As she opened the door to the loading area, she was met by the familiar sounds of the manual-labor end of a newspaper: people bustling to and from, dollies and forklifts jockeying for position, engines idling and horns honking. "Hi, Rachel!" called an older woman who was already helping to load up her drivers. "You come down to slum with us workin' stiffs?"

As she walked passed the woman, Rachel gave her a quick hug.
"You just let me know when you want to trade jobs, June!" Moving on, Rachel called over her shoulder, "Hi, Howard! Hi, Pookie!"
Pookie, June's Yorkshire terrier, anxiously supervised the proceedings from the passenger's side of a white van, where June's husband Howard sat, ready to roll. Rachel shook her head. What a family! Howard and June's daughter, Missy, had worked for The

Evergreen News years ago and had persuaded her parents to help out one night when the drivers had gone on strike. Little did she know they would think it was fun. For the last seven years, Howard — an overweight smoker who was a heart attack waiting to happen had been a bundle driver and assistant to June, who had scored a job as district manager. They were good-hearted people and Rachel genuinely liked them, although she was afraid the job would kill them both.

Rachel strode to the far side of the loading dock where she could see several bundle-drop drivers loading their vans. She walked over to her two new hires, Bud and Jim, and gave them directions on what they needed to do. For the next thirty minutes, organized chaos reigned, until finally the bay was quiet, the drivers loaded and, on their way, to meet the hundreds of carriers around the city.

However, one large stack of papers remained, and Rachel knew exactly which driver they belonged to.

Rachel had known from the beginning that she shouldn't hire Sacha. He was tall, lean, and beautiful, his kinky caramel hair and aquamarine eyes betraying a mixed heritage, a philosopher who concerned himself with the more intangible and important questions of life. Rachel had predicted that the repetitions task of following the same route, day in-day out, would not be for him. The right thing to do would have been to reject his application, but the truth was that she had fallen prey to his charisma. Not that she imagined herself involved with him — but she did look forward to running into him down on the dock, listening to his gentle musings, drinking in his unusually spiritual persona.

But here it was, 3:40 P.M. on a Wednesday afternoon, 10,000 papers had to get out, and there was no Sacha, which meant that Rachel would have to quickly find someone to fill in for him.

For the second time that day, she swore.

CHAPTER 3

Saturday morning dawned sunny and warm, the sky boasting a brilliant blue, an aftermath to a cleansing rain. David rose early and, as he did first thing every morning, he moved to the exercise mat in the living room of his waterfront condominium, positioning himself directly in front of the sliding glass doors. Then, as he gazed out at the sound and the islands beyond, he went through a series of gentle stretching exercises. He loved starting his day this way, as though he were awakening both his mental and physical selves, preparing his mind and body for whatever might come his way.

When finished, he opened one of the oak-paneled kitchen cupboards where dozens of bottles of diet supplements stood neatly organized. Quickly choosing what he needed, David mixed himself a protein drink, which he downed quickly, followed by a concoction that blended carbohydrates, amino acids, and vitamins. Finally, he sliced and quartered a grapefruit, which he ate standing over the sink.

At eight-thirty, he locked the door and traversed the twenty feet of trellised breezeway to his neatly kept garage where his Dodge van and BMW awaited. Choosing the latter for this morning's trip, he set out for the nearby hamlet of Oakbrook, where the local health food store was sponsoring a two-day seminar on food supplements and optimum health by a well-known nutritionist.

Ten minutes later, when David swung the Beemer into the parking lot of Heart and Mind Health, he was surprised to find it almost completely filled. He finally steered his car into a space next to an older Jaguar, polished to a sheen that brought out the fine gold detailing on the classic racing-green finish. When he paused a moment to admire it as he walked by, he could see someone on the back seat, head down, evidently searching for something on the floor. He quickly moved away and headed toward the store, rounding the outside of the building and entering a side door which he knew would lead him to the conference room in the rear.

The line for registration had already formed, and David took his place at the end behind an overweight woman wearing a bright coral sweatshirt and matching leggings. She turned to give him a quick appraisal, her long hoop earrings swinging wildly at the sudden movement. Then she smiled coyly.

"Hi," she cooed, her voice tinged with a Southern accent. "Looks like it's gonna be a while before we get in there."

"Yes, it does," responded David courteously, but his manner clearly communicated that he didn't care to engage in small talk.

Seeing that their conversation was over, the woman's smile faded, and she turned back to face toward the front of the line. David retreated into his own thoughts, wondering if the speaker was as good as the size of the crowd would indicate.

People continued to join the line, and within a few minutes it reached all the way to the door. One woman, however, did not stop to take a place at the line's end but eased her way past those waiting and headed straight for the lady in the coral outfit.

"Thanks for saving my spot," she said, and with a glance over her shoulder, she asked David, "You don't mind, do you?"

David stared at the woman, speechless. She had deep brown eyes, high cheekbones, smooth olive skin, and sleek black hair that hung halfway down her back.

The new woman took David's silence to be a form of protest. "I just had to run out to my car to get my notebook," she explained, holding up a spiral-bound tablet as evidence. "I have such a poor memory, I was afraid I wouldn't remember it all when I got home."

David stood mutely, just gazing into the woman's eyes. Still thinking he was unhappy with her maneuver, she became a little irritated. "Really," she insisted, "I was here before you.

David realized that he needed to say something. "No, no — that's fine," he assured the woman. She gave him a long look, and then turned toward the registration desk to await her turn.

David continued to stare at her back. Could it be? Was this the woman who haunted his dreams, whose image seemed indelibly printed upon his soul? He realized he was holding his breath, a tautness in his gut making it hard for him to breathe.

Lost in his thoughts, David vaguely heard the raised voice of a mother trying to subdue her three adolescents' sons who stood just behind him in line.

"Stop it, Will. Josh, you stand over there. Bret, you stay right here."

"Yeah, Brat!" sneered one of his siblings. "You stay right there with Mommy!

Bret evidently took exception to having his name taken in vain, for he broke away from his mother's grasp and gave his brother a shove —right into David.

Thrown off balance by the unexpected bump, David instinctively put out his hands to keep from knocking over the people in front of him. Unfortunately, those hands found themselves innocently, but firmly, planted on the buttocks of the beautiful brunette. She whirled around instantly and gave David a quick, stinging, no-nonsense slap.

"Wait!" protested David, holding up his hands to ward off another blow.

The woman gave him a piercing look, her eyes filled with fire and fury.

"Just what the hell are you doing?" she snapped.

"Oh, God, I'm sorry," apologized David, mortified by what he had done. "But I couldn't help it. These kids were horsing around, and they shoved me into you."

He turned around to show her the true culprits who, unfortunately, were no longer there. Instead, David caught a glimpse of their retreating backs as mother and sons made a guilty dash toward the parking lot.

"I don't see any kids," the woman pointed out.
David brought his gaze back to her and found himself distracted by the attractive flush of pink highlighting her cheekbones.

"I guess they left," he said, and his excuse sounded lame even to his ears. "But I am telling the truth. I would never. he searched for an inoffensive word for butt grabbing and came up empty ...do that on purpose. I'm very, very sorry."

"Next!" The man at the registration desk shouted in their direction. In all the commotion, David and the woman had failed to notice the line moving forward. She turned on her heel, marched up to the desk, paid her fee, and moved into the conference room without looking back.

Once David had registered, he walked tentatively toward the door to the conference room where he peered inside cautiously. He searched for the telltale mane of black hair and finally found the woman sitting on the left side of the room. He chose a seat on the right side, sitting as far away from her as possible.

For the next two hours, however, David could barely concentrate on anything but the striking woman with the dark eyes and raven hair. There was no denying that he was drawn to her, his eyes unconsciously seeking her out several times during the lecture. And more than once he found her staring back at him, a wary look clouding her expressive eyes.

What tricks fate does play, thought David unhappily. I unexpectedly find the woman I've been longing for, searching for, yet our meeting couldn't have been more awkward and unpleasant — certainly not the way I'd envisioned meeting my soulmate.

At the conclusion of the lecture, David was the first one out the door, making sure he avoided another encounter with the woman. He loped to his car, where he quickly unlocked the door, slid behind the wheel, and gunned the engine. He was out of the parking lot and heading down the road just as people started coming out of the side door.

As he lay in bed that night, he thought about what he would do the following morning to once again explain what happened to somehow win the woman's forgiveness. This was one area in which he felt woefully inadequate, an inexperienced player when it came to the games that men and women play. Although he had had his share of girlfriends, a few of them serious, he had never learned the art of flirting, of using guile to win a woman's trust and affection.

His approach had always been disconcertingly straightforward, simply admitting how he felt and hoping that his feelings would be reciprocated. He knew no charming little tricks, no clever lines nor contrived circumstances that would help him get back in the black-haired beauty's good graces.

As he fell into a fitful sleep, he came to the decision that all he could do was be himself and hope that that would be enough.

Sunday morning brought clear skies once again, their blue more muted than the day before.

Once again, David started his day with his regular routine, albeit a little earlier. He planned to be the first one at the seminar this morning so that he could intercept the woman and once again apologize. If things went well, perhaps he would learn her name, even sit next to her and get to know her a bit.

When David arrived this time, he had no trouble finding a place to park. In fact, the only other car in the lot was the vintage Jag, probably the instructor's car, he thought. However, when he tried the side door of the health food store, he found that it was still locked. He circled around to the front of the store where he entered through the front doors and headed straight to the counter. A young woman sat behind the cash register putting tags on bottles with a price gun.

"Good morning," he said. "I'm here for this morning's seminar, but I couldn't get in through the side door.

"Yeah, the guy in charge hasn't shown yet," she told him without missing a bottle. "You'll have to wait till he gets here to open up the conference room." Finishing her task, she nodded her head in the direction of the book rack where a woman stood reading. "At least you have some company. You're our second early bird today."

Following her gaze, David turned to find the woman of his dreams standing there. Just at that moment, she looked up, and for a moment their eyes held. David felt a strange but pleasant shiver run down his spine.

Then the woman's face broke out into a big smile.

"Hi!" she said. "I'm so glad you're here. I came early, hoping to catch you — She flushed prettily, and then picked up her notebook and walked over to David. "I just wanted to apologize for yesterday.

I shouldn't have slapped you. After I came to my senses, I realized you weren't the kind of guy who goes around grabbing innocent girls' behinds."

As her eyes searched his earnestly, David was once again captivated by her looks — the shiny hair, the huge brown eyes, the flawless skin — she was The Black.

"I understand how you must have felt," he said. "And I don't blame you at all. It was completely my fault, and I really am sorry."

"Thank you," she said, lowering her eyes for a moment, then she extended her hand. "My name is Rachel."

David took her hand, clasping it firmly and perhaps a little longer than necessary. "I'm David."

"Can I buy you a cup of coffee, David? To show you there are no hard feelings?"

"I'd like that," he replied, "but it's my treat — the least I can do for... bumping into you."

Gently putting his hand on Rachel's elbow, he guided her to a small, wrought-iron table with two chairs squeezed into a corner of the store. A nearby sideboard held a carafe of gourmet coffee from which he poured two cups. After dropping a few bills into the collection box, he delivered the steaming cups, along with an assortment of cream and sugar packets, to the table.

Rachel opened two of the cream packets and emptied them into her cup. For a few moments, David did nothing but watch her, amazed at how much she reminded him of the woman in his fantasy. Then, realizing that he was staring, he tended to the business of preparing his coffee, opening the remaining two cream packets and pouring them into his coffee.

An awkward silence hovered for a moment as each tried to think of something to say. David spoke first.

"I appreciate you taking the trouble to come early to talk to me. Most people would have avoided me or, worse, given me a piece of their mind."

Rachel laughed. "Well, I gave you a piece yesterday, and that's about all I can spare." She took another sip of her coffee. "The truth is, if I think someone's out of line, I can get real mad really quick. On the other hand, if I think I've made a mistake, I like to set it right. I may end up doing a lot of apologizing, but at least people always know where they stand with me. " She looked straight into David's eyes, her lips parted a bit so that her even white teeth contrasted attractively against her full, red lips.

"No games," said David, nodding. "That's how I like to operate too.

With this admission they both relaxed and fell into easy conversation about a variety of topics. Rachel laughed often and easily; David smiled more than he had for months, simply enjoying being in the company of such a beautiful and intelligent woman.

Before they knew it, the girl at the cash register called, "Hey, you two, the seminar's about to start. You'd better get in there."

"Whoops!" laughed Rachel and stood up quickly. As she did so, a ring of keys fell out of the side pocket of her purse. David stooped to pick them up, noticing that a small, worn, silver cross dangled from the key ring, along with a dozen or so keys. Again, the shiver traveled down his back, but he said nothing as he handed the keys back to Rachel.

Quickly, they walked through the store, across the foyer, and into the conference room, where the speaker was already delivering his opening remarks. Everyone appeared to be in the same seats they had occupied the day before. Rachel gave David a little wave and walked around to her seat on the left side of the room. As much as David wanted to follow, he didn't feel confident enough to do so. He moved right and slid into his seat.

As had happened the day before, the information from the seminar was lost on David as he spent the next two hours thinking about Rachel, trying not to constantly look in her direction. Every once in a while, their eyes would connect, and David would feel a charge of electricity surge through his body. How could someone he just met, whom he barely knew, make him feel so alive? Of course, the answer was that he had known her in his heart, his mind, his soul for a long time.

By the end of the lecture, David had rehearsed to perfection how he would walk over to Rachel and invite her to go get something to eat. As he started across the room, however, a tall woman with frizzy blonde hair approached Rachel and tapped her on the arm.

"Ginny!" he could here Rachel exclaim. "How are you? Have you been here the whole time?"

David couldn't hear Ginny's reply, but he could tell by their animated conversation that the two women knew each other well. Oh well, he thought, I'll just hang around the store until Ginny leaves and then ask Rachel to lunch.

But Ginny didn't leave by herself. She and Rachel, deep in conversation, left the conference room together. Rachel never looked back, didn't even think to wave goodbye to David, never gave him an opportunity to learn her last name, much less her phone number.

At a discreet distance, he followed the women out to the parking lot, where Rachel unlocked the driver's side of the classic green Jaguar and climbed in behind the wheel; Ginny got in on the passenger's side. As David watched them drive out of the lot, he felt a great loss.

How could Rachel completely forget about him like that, just leave without any thought of him, when he had felt so connected to her?

There was only one answer: Perhaps she wasn't The Black after all.

CHAPTER 4

It was almost four o'clock on the first Friday in June when David and Terry checked into the Windswept Inn on the outskirts of Ellensburg. They had just come across Snoqualmie Pass, traversing the mountains at a leisurely pace so they could enjoy the view: mountain meadows, lush and green, dusted with the first crop of wildflowers; dozens of waterfalls, from timid little trickles to thundering cascades; glacier-covered peaks that seemed to impale the deep blue sky. It had been a spectacular ride.

The Windswept Inn did not offer a lot of amenities, but it was clean, comfortable and quiet. When Terry and David registered, the clerk, a fair-haired, scrawny young man who couldn't have been more than eighteen, looked at them with open-mouthed awe.

"You must be here for the powerlifting meet," he ventured, eyeing Terry's bulging biceps.

"Sure am," replied Terry, giving the kid a friendly smile.

"Are you gonna come watch?"

"Nah," he said, looking down at the registration form. "My dad says it's a waste of time. He'll probably make me work anyway."

Clearly the boy did not share his dad's opinion. Terry looked at him with benevolent amusement.

"How much do you weigh, kid?" he asked.

The boy reddened and stood up straighter. "Some days I get up to a hundred and forty."

"Well, I used to weigh one-forty myself," said Terry. He took out his wallet and withdrew two tickets. "Here's a couple of passes for tomorrow, just in case you don't have to work. That way at least your dad can't say you're wasting your money.

The boy hesitated, then took the passes, giving Terry a grateful look.

"And you keep up with those weights," Terry called over his shoulder as he and David went out the door.

"When were you ever a hundred and forty pounds?" asked David as they walked to their room.

"When I was twelve," answered Terry innocently.

The two men unpacked and then drove into town for an early dinner at a restaurant Terry knew. Unlike most other athletes, powerlifters don't need to watch their diet; instead, they eat what they want and typically carry a few extra pounds, which helps increase the weight load they can carry. While David ordered a healthy dinner of chicken tarragon, wild rice, and Caesar salad, Terry bulked up on a 20-ounce porterhouse, baked potato with sour cream and bacon, broccoli smothered in hollandaise sauce, a basket of sourdough bread, and chocolate cream pie for dessert.

Afterward, the two men headed back to the motel where they turned in early to get a good night's rest.

As he drifted off to sleep, David saw the familiar figure of The Black in his mind's eye. She was standing on the ridge of a hill, looking out across a valley. As usual, her back was to him, and he could see only her ebony hair flowing in the wind.

This time, however, she turned and gazed directly into his eyes, sending an electric charge shuddering through his body. He had waited so long for her identity to be revealed, and now that he could finally see her face, he realized he knew who she was.

The next morning David and Terry took their time getting ready for the day, each man going through his own routine. After they checked out of the motel, they returned to the same restaurant for breakfast. Once again, Terry ate well, enjoying the blue-plate special of eggs, toast, hash browns and sausage.

"So, who's your competition today?" asked David, sucking the juice out of his grapefruit rind.

"Sobeck, probably. But I don't think he can touch me."

"Sobeck? Doesn't he do steroids? I thought this was a natural meet."

Terry sighed. "Well, it is, in theory." Idly he swished the ice around in his water glass with a spoon. "The meet's sanctioned by the American Powerlifting Federation, but they don't require testing, so anyone — on any damn drug — can enter.

He spooned an ice cube into his mouth and began to crunch. "You can always tell which guys are using drugs," he sputtered, chunks of ice flying out of his mouth as he spoke. "They get an attitude. They become aggressive and lose their judgment. Those are the guys I want you to watch out for today."

"What about Carlisle?" David asked. "I thought he was the guy who came closest to matching your numbers.'

Terry gave a little laugh. "Yeah, well, he let his numbers go to his head. He's got a broken leg." The way Terry revealed this bit of news made it plain that there was more to the story.

"What happened?" asked David. "Someone break it for him? Dropped a weight on it maybe?" That was just the kind of stunt Terry had brought David along to prevent.

"Nah, he did it himself. He was down in northern California at some kind of powerlifters' get-together, and he was braggin' about how much weight he could carry on his squats. Evidently, some guy challenged him to a grudge match. Carlisle loaded up too much and pop! His femur snapped and stuck right out of his thigh!" A guffaw erupted from Terry's lips before he could swallow it. "I know it's not funny, and I don't like to see anyone get hurt," he said, looking sheepish, "but Carlisle just asks for it."

They paid the bill and climbed into Terry's car for the short drive to the Ellensburg Rodeo, the site of the powerlifting meet. Although they arrived about an hour before the meet was to start, several of the other contestants were already there.

Terry and David made their way to the Quonset hut that served as the staging area. At the registration desk sat two women with placards in front of them reading "A — M" and "N — Z." Walking up to the second woman, whose name tag identified her as Jill, Terry introduced himself.

"Oh, Mr. Patrick," she bubbled, "it's such a thrill to meet you." She had rich auburn hair, gray-green eyes, and a turned-up nose sprinkled with freckles — altogether an all-American, freshly scrubbed, very attractive face.

"The pleasure is mine," countered Terry, and for a moment they just gazed at each other in mutual admiration.

Suddenly, the woman remembered her job. "Oh, here's your registration packet and a T-shirt with all the participants' names on it." She flashed a sunny smile. "Good luck," she said, and then with a flirtatious wink she added, "although I doubt, you'll need it."

Terry thanked her, and he and David moved into the staging area where they found a quiet corner to prepare for the meet. David helped Terry into his powerlifting suit — similar to that worn by a wrestler, but so snug that it took two people to squeeze the lifter into it. It wasn't vanity but necessity that made the suit so tight; the snugness provided essential support to the body during the stress of the lifts.

Terry began his warm-up routine nothing too strenuous but enough to prepare his body for the grueling workout it was about to endure. David stood to one side, helping Terry when he could, but mainly keeping an eye on the other people in the Quonset hut — no easy feat as there were nearly two hundred contestants.

At one point, a burly man with a shaved head and a gold ring in his ear walked by and then stopped.

"I'm gonna get you today, Patrick," he told Terry. Although he clearly meant to sound as though he were kidding Terry, his voice held an edge to it, a threat implied in the words.

"Well, you just might, Sobeck, if you're still using that hi-test stuff," replied Terry with a small smile. He was referring to the steroid testosterone which some powerlifters took to enhance their performance.

"Shit," spat the man, no longer any trace of friendliness in his voice. "I don't need that to beat a has-been like you."
Giving Terry a malevolent glare, he stomped off.

"Jeez, am I over the hill and nobody told me?" asked Terry in mock surprise. Besides being an easygoing guy, Terry never took to heart what other competitors said to him. He knew they were trying to rev themselves up to give the performance of their lives. Different lifters used different techniques. Some sniffed ammonia, which cleared the brain of all thoughts, so they could focus only on the lift. Others had their spotters slap them around, the idea being that this would anger the lifter enough to get his adrenaline surging. Terry didn't believe in using artificial motivators, and David thought the slapping frenzies were used mainly to excite the audience, much like pro wrestling.

Finally, the meet began, and groups of men traipsed out of the hut and onto the stage as their weight class was called. There were three divisions: teenage, open, and masters. Because he was over forty, Terry could enter both the open and the masters, often setting records in the latter class.
Finally, it was time for the 245-pound class in the open division of the bench press. Terry and David walked out to the stage where they were joined by several other powerlifters and spotters.

Each contestant in the bench press was given three tries to lift more weight than his competitors. The officials started with 225 pounds on the bench press bar. Those who wanted to lift stepped forward; if they completed a successful lift, they remained in the competition, but with only two lifts left. After everyone who wanted to lift at that weight had done so, the officials added more plates to the bar, announced the new weight, and asked those who wanted to lift to step forward.

The rules of the bench press were very strict. One of the two spotters was allowed to stand over the lifter and help ease the bar off the holder and into his hands. Once the lifter took full control, the spotter moved quickly to the side of the bench press. The lifter then lowered the bar to a dead stop just above his chest and waited for the officials to give the signal to lift. If he couldn't make the lift, the spotters' job was to keep the weight from falling back onto the lifter and crushing his chest.

Even if a contestant failed to make the lift on his first or second try, he wasn't disqualified but simply penalized by losing his turn. He could still use the other attempts he had coming to him to lift the bar, but he would have to match or exceed the last weight lifted. And if a spotter mistakenly grabbed the bar before the completion of the lift, the same rules applied: a foul would be called, and, again, the lifter would lose one of his lifts.

The field was strong at this particular event, and no one stepped forward to lift until the bar was at 415 pounds. With each increase of weight, lifters were eliminated. But not Terry. He didn't even try his first lift until the weight reached 585 pounds — which no doubt cracked the confidence of the few remaining competitors, most of whom had already used two of their three lifts by then.

As Terry took his place on the bench, he looked up at the second spotter who had been provided by the tournament to assist David. He was young and inexperienced and somewhat intimidated by Terry's fame and prowess.

Terry, nice guy that he was, became deadly serious in competition. He fixed the spotter with a steely stare and said, "I appreciate you being here to spot for me. But get this straight: If you touch the bar and disqualify me, I'll kick your ass."

The Adam's apple moved up and down on the spotter's neck, and he nodded to show he understood. More than one spotter had been bribed to fix an event, but it wasn't going to happen to Terry, not today.

Terry lifted the 585 pounds easily. On the next go around, the rest of the competitors were eliminated, except for one Sobeck. The two men glared at each other, each choosing to wait until the bar held 645 pounds to try again. Both succeeded. Now they were down to their third and final lift.

Sobeck stepped forward at 695 pounds. He pushed, he grunted, he raised the bar half way, and then, exhaling with such force that he sounded like a balloon deflating, Sobeck let his arms go slack. His spotters caught the bar; he had failed.

Terry took his place and reached for the bar. Down it went and then back up again, steady as a rock. Once the bar had been lifted on him, Terry stood up and lifted his arms in victory to the crowd, which showed its appreciation with wild applause. Then he walked over to Sobeck and extended his hand; the other man, however, threw his towel on the floor and stomped.

Terry and David returned to the staging area to await the master's event. It was in the master's that Terry usually went for a record. Since the field was smaller and the competition not as tough, he could generally win the event on his second lift and use his third to go for a record.

Terry won his class in the master's easily with a lift of 645 pounds. Then he gave a sign to the officials, and the announcer came on the P.A. system.

"Ladies and gentlemen, Terry Patrick will try to set the record on his third lift with a weight of 715 pounds."

An excited murmur ran through the crowd. This is what they came to see, sheer brawn and determination defying the laws of nature.

Terry lay down on the bench. David and the assistant spotter grunted under the weight of the bar as they handed it off to Terry. Terry brought the bar down slowly and waited.

"Lift," came the official's signal.

Slowly, the bar came up. David watched anxiously, knowing Terry had never attempted so much weight. The bar inched upward; Terry's face grew red, veins popping out on his neck and forehead. Suddenly he began gasping for air and the bar started to drop.

David grabbed his end and screamed "Catch it!" to the other spotter. Instead, the spotter backed off, confused and scared into inaction by Terry's earlier threat.

Thinking quickly, David shoved his end of the bar upward with all his might as the spotter's end crashed to the floor. The transfer of weight made the bar hurtle end-over-end onto the wooden platform, where it left a sizable hole.

Although David had saved Terry from a crushed sternum, the lifter was unconscious and still in grave danger. David pulled Terry's limp body onto the floor and immediately started CPR. "Call the paramedics!" he instructed the dazed spotter.

An official knelt beside him. "They're on their way."

Within two minutes the paramedics had arrived and taken over the CPR. Then, placing Terry carefully on a gurney, they loaded him into an ambulance for the short ride to Memorial Hospital.

Before they could close the rear doors to the ambulance, David jumped in and buckled himself into a seat belt.

"I'm coming with you," he insisted. When one of the medics began to protest, David said, "You'll need someone to do the paperwork."

They rushed off to the hospital where Terry was sent to the intensive care unit. David checked in at administration and was given a stack of forms to fill out. Once finished, he hurried down the slick, white halls to ICU, where he approached the information desk, manned this afternoon by an older woman with curly gray hair.

"What's happening with Terry Patrick? Can I see him?' he asked.

The nurse peered at him over her bifocals.

"Are you a relative?" she asked skeptically.

"His brother, David Patrick."

"I see," she said, though she didn't look like she believed him. "The doctors are with him now. We'll let you know." She waved David toward the waiting room.

David sat down next to an elderly black man who gave him a sympathetic smile. "Better get used to it," he advised. "I've been here for four hours, and nobody's told me nothin."

Suddenly, a young woman rushed into the waiting room and looked around anxiously. David recognized her as Jill, the woman who had checked them in at the meet.

She spied David and hurried over to him.

"I heard Terry Patrick collapsed," she said. "What happened? Is he going to be okay?"

"He went into cardiac arrest while he was going for the record in the bench press. The doctors are working on him now, but I don't know anything yet."

"Oh." She looked uncertain. "Mind if I wait a while with you?"

"That'd be nice," smiled David.

They waited for over two hours. Finally, a man dressed in white came out of the double doors and walked over to them.

"You're waiting for Terry Patrick?" he asked. When David nodded, he said, "He's had a heart attack. We've got him stabilized, but we're going to have to keep him here for a bit, four or five days at least." He looked at David and Jill. "You're his relatives?"

"Brother," lied David.

Jill didn't miss a beat. "Sister."

"All right, you can see him, but just for a couple of minutes. Okay?"

David entered the room first. Tubes stuck out of Terry every which way and he looked pale and weak.

"Jeez, Terry, you scared the hell out of me," David said softly.

"Hey, buddy," said Terry and gave him a smile. "You're one hell of a bodyguard. The doctor says you probably saved my life." He paused for a moment to catch his breath. "This isn't exactly what I had in mind when I brought you along."

"Hey, I'll just put it on the bill," said David with a grin. "Looks like you're going to be okay, but they want to keep you here for a while." He glanced over to the door and motioned Jill to come in. "I've got someone here who wants to say hello."

Jill walked in hesitantly. "Hi, Mr. Patrick." She looked at David who nodded encouragingly. "I heard what happened at the meet and thought I'd just come over to wish you well."

Terry looked at her with happy surprise. "That is so sweet. And, please, call me Terry. Especially if you're going to be visiting me while I'm here the next few days."

The worried look on Jill's face dissolved into a sunny smile. "Alright... Terry. You take care and I'll see you tomorrow."

Jill gave David a lift back to the Ellensburg Rodeo where he packed up Terry's car and headed back home. He would call the hospital daily to see how Terry was doing and then return to pick him up when he was released.

On the drive back, he thought about how Jill and Terry had just hit it off, found each other suddenly, randomly, made a connection that only chemistry can explain.

He thought that had happened to him, too, when he had met Rachel at the health food store. But she evidently hadn't shared his feelings, having left without so much as a goodbye.

And now it was her face he saw when he dreamt of The Black.

CHAPTER 5

"Okay, next up is Rachel."

Rachel all eyes turned to Rachel, who was sitting at the far end of the conference table. She was leaning forward, her right elbow on the table, her hand cupping her chin. In her other hand she held a pencil, which she spun around absently on the slick formica veneer, a vacant, faraway look in her eye. Wherever she was, she was completely oblivious to the business being conducted at the monthly staff meeting of The Evergreen News.

"Rachel?"

Rudely jerked out of her reverie, Rachel sat up with a start. She saw that the vice president, who conducted the meetings, and everyone else sitting around the table were staring at her expectantly. Some faces held benign amusement; others simply looked bored. Only one face showed annoyance that of Evan, the pompous business manager, who tapped his gold-plated fountain pen impatiently.

"Oh... I . . . uh... I've got it right here," stammered Rachel. Quickly she turned to her notes and gave a quick report on the personnel department figures for the past month. This was not the first time she had been caught daydreaming; in fact, her frequent bouts of inattention were so common they were the subject of many an office joke. She took the ribbing in stride, thankful that her coworkers made light of her problem rather than castigating her for it.

Ever since she could remember, Rachel had had a problem keeping her mind on any one thing for very long. It had caused her no end of trouble in school. Every teacher she'd known had accused her of being inattentive, even though she had been smart enough to get A's and B's in most of her classes. That was before medical science had discovered ADD — attention deficit disorder — and parents and teachers realized that lots of children suffered from this abnormality. Even though there were now drugs available to ease the problem, Rachel refused to take them. She didn't like to put anything unnatural in her body, and she had decided long ago that she could learn to live with this small imperfection.

However, this morning she found herself cursing her inability to concentrate, for it had cost her something that might be important — getting to know a man whom she knew only as David.

That was what she had been thinking about during the meeting — how she had hoped to talk to David after the seminar at the health food store, but then she had run into her friend Ginny, who had asked for a ride home, and her

mind had just suddenly switched gears. Typically, it was when something unexpected happened to her that she was most likely to forget what she was doing. But how could she have forgotten someone like David? Even though she had spent less than half an hour talking with him, she had felt they shared a rare connection, not only intellectually but sexually. When she thought of him now, she could feel the fine hairs on the back of her neck bristle with tension.

She had done what she could to find him, calling the health food store the next day and asking for David's phone number.

"I'm afraid we can't give that out," came the slightly shocked reply. "What if you were some stalker? I'm sorry, but we really couldn't invade his privacy."

Rachel didn't appreciate being likened to a lovesick wacko and tried another tack.

"Oh, no, you don't understand. It's just that I've got a book of his, one he lent me and expects back. But I've lost his phone number and he doesn't know mine, so I have no idea how to get in touch with him to return it." Once again, Rachel felt she would have to rely on creativity rather than the truth if she were to get results.

"Oh. . . well...," the clerk sounded more doubtful. "Just a minute." Evidently the woman had put her hand over the receiver for Rachel could hear the sound of muffled conversation. Then, "Well, it doesn't matter, because the man who conducted the seminar has that information, not us. Do you want his business number?"

Rachel dutifully called New Trition Enterprises but learned that the seminar leader was on a five-state lecture tour and wouldn't be back in the office for several weeks. She could try back then.

And so, she had no idea when she would be seeing David again, if ever.

Later, as she sat in her phone-booth sized office reviewing employment applications, Rachel heard a tap tap. She looked up to see Ken, one of the district managers, standing there.

"Ken, hi, come on in," invited Rachel. She hastily cleared a stack of papers off the only other chair in her office.

"Don't mind if I do," said Ken, as he eased into the office, quietly closing the door behind him.

"Hey," cried Rachel, in mock alarm. "What are you planning to do? Ravage me?"

"Don't you wish," teased Ken, sliding into the chair.

"Well, if that's not the reason we're incommunicado, then you must have something juicy to tell me. Spill it."

Rachel liked and trusted Ken something she couldn't say about many of the other district managers at The Evergreen News. Ken came from a newspaper family and knew the business well. He had been a good friend to Rachel, acting as her mentor when she had first come to the paper. And, although Rachel found Ken handsome in a geeky sort of way, and she knew he thought she was attractive, their relationship had remained blissfully platonic, due in part, no doubt, to the fact that Ken was happily married to Kara, a dynamic woman with lots of personality and energy. With her around, Ken didn't need any outside entertainment.

Ken leaned toward Rachel and spoke in a conspiratorial tone.

"I've got a couple of tidbits for you," he confided. "First, and you are the first to know, I'm moving on."

"What? Oh, no! Don't leave me here alone," begged Rachel. "Who wants you, anyway?" Rachel knew that Ken was seriously underpaid at the News given his background and expertise, and she had long feared he would escape to a better position somewhere else.

"Well, I'm movin' on up to the big time — as in The Seattle Times." There was little love for the Times at The Evergreen News. The local paper had provided some competition to the Times in the south Puget Sound area, so the Times had recently made a deal to acquire it. Those in the know felt that it was just a matter of time until the parent company ran its baby out of business.

"Traitor!" accused Rachel. "I suppose they gave you a better job with more money. Like that's a good reason to leave!"

"They did," admitted Ken. "But there's another reason I took the job. Rachel, I think the rumors are true: The News isn't going to be around much longer."

Rachel sat back in her chair, the better to digest this news. "Really. Have you found something out?

"A few things. First of all, Bill Wick is hooked on prescription drugs," he said, referring to the publisher. "He's made some wild decisions that have really hurt our credibility in this market. Circulation numbers are on a downward spiral. And then there's the recycling scam."

As Ken explained it, one of the district managers, John Sanborne, also operated a recycling station. On the two days each week that The Evergreen News was supposed to be delivered to 235,000 additional nonpaying customers — courtesy of the many advertisers who paid for inserts —John had found a way to divert those papers, undelivered, to his recycling station.

"That's fraud!" exclaimed Rachel, incredulously.

"Yeah, it's pretty stupid, and he's going to get caught. But between John's scam and Bill's bad habit, I'd say the News is going down real soon."

Rachel contemplated all of this as she drove home that evening. Her meditative state kept her from speeding, which was a good thing since a cop car happened to be traveling behind her for several miles. Finally, the cruiser pulled around the Jaguar and passed it. Just as it did, a cigarette butt, still smoking, flew out of the window and bounced on the hood of the Jaguar.

That got Rachel's attention.

"Hey!" she yelled. "Hey, you!"

The patrol car continued to pull away from her, the officers oblivious to her shouts. Rachel pulled up behind their car and started honking her horn and flashing her headlights.

"Pull over!" she shouted.

The patrolman who was driving finally looked in his rear-view mirror and realized what Rachel wanted. When it was safe to do so, he pulled the car over to the shoulder of the road. The officer in the passenger's seat, the one who had tossed the cigarette butt, got out of the car and was making his way back to the Jaguar when Rachel, who had jumped out of her car as soon as it had stopped, intercepted him.

"What do you think you're doing, throwing a cigarette, a lit cigarette, out of your window?" demanded Rachel, her face flushed with fury. "Not only is that against the law, not only is that dangerous, it's rude!"

The officer looked at Rachel in amazement, and then a grin crept slowly onto his face.

"You!" gasped Rachel. She recognized him as the cop who had pulled her over for putting her makeup on in the car. "You ought to know better! Why on earth would you do that?"

The policeman thought for a moment. "Well, you see, my wife doesn't know I still smoke and if she finds out, she'll divorce me. I can't put my cigarette out in the car's ashtray, because I drive this car home and she'll check it for butts and bust me. I've got two small children and I love my wife, so I don't want to break up my family, but I just can't seem to quit..." his voice trailed off, but his gaze held steadily on Rachel, the grin still in place.

Rachel had to laugh. "All right, we're even. I'll let you off this time, but no more fiery butts on the roadside, okay?"

The policeman nodded. "And you're on this road every day, so you'll be watching me, I know.

"You bet I will." She gave the policeman a long look, noticing not for the first time that he was tall, well-built, and attractive. "Why don't you just give up that filthy habit? You don't need it."

"And you don't need makeup."

Rachel flushed at the compliment. "Touché."

Back in her car, Rachel continued the drive homeward, thinking about the handsome cop. He seemed like a nice guy, certainly was good-looking, and had a sense of humor, but Rachel could never be attracted to someone who smoked. She thought about Michael, whom she cared for and had almost married. Another nice guy who had gobs of money and was crazy about her. But for Rachel, there was something missing; she had never felt that indefinable but palpable feeling of irresistible attraction to Michael. She sighed. The world was full of good guys, but she wanted something more. She wanted a lion.

Like most prepubescent girls, Rachel had created romantic fantasies when she was younger, dreaming of living happily ever after with a handsome prince of a man. Over the years, however, as she matured, she had begun to reflect on her dream man's character as well as his looks. Somewhere along the line she had come to think of her perfect mate as a lion — strong, confident, independent, intelligent, beautiful.

Rachel wanted someone who made her blood run hot, whose company she enjoyed whether in conversation or in bed, someone who took risks but never compromised his integrity. Why was he so difficult to find?

Her thoughts turned back to David. She barely knew him and yet she was beginning to wonder if perhaps he might be just that kind of a man.

Had she missed her only chance to ever find out?

CHAPTER 6

"Trans Pacific Sales."

"Uh, yeah, you a liquidator?"

"Yep. Have you got something to unload?"

David listened intently as the man on the other end of the line described his merchandise. He had 2500 stuffed animals, talking bunnies that were supposed to be a famous cartoon character, except they were missing the bunny's trademark teeth. Could David get rid of them?

"Well, that depends," said David. "Since they don't really look like Bucky Bunny, they're a risky bet. I could get burned." He paused, letting the caller worry a bit. "I'll tell you what. I'll gamble and give you a dollar a piece for them." "What? They retail for $24.99!"

Not without the teeth they don't, thought David. To the caller he said, "There's no guarantee I can sell them at any price, and if I can't move them, I'm out $2500." He knew his price was low, but he didn't care if he lost this particular deal.

The man muttered an insulting remark, but David remained cool.

"Listen, I've got another call coming in," he said. "Why don't you think about it and call me back?"

David disconnected and sat back in his chair. There was no incoming call, but he had wanted to get off the phone quickly for a couple of reasons. First, by ending the call abruptly, he had created a sense of urgency for the seller; and, second, he hadn't wanted to listen to the caller vent about how he was getting screwed. David understood that many of the people he talked to were under stress, and he was genuinely empathetic; more than once he had bumped up his bid because he felt sorry for the guy on the other end of the phone.

But if a seller started to get abusive, he usually terminated negotiations. After all, this was a business; sellers, buyers, and middlemen — which is where David fit in — were all trying to get the best deal they could. If someone took it as a personal affront when he offered a low price for a nearly unsaleable item, he would just as soon not work with them.

He barely had the phone back in its cradle when it rang again.

"Trans Pacific Sales."

"Yeah, Dick Sloane said for me, to call you,' came a man's voice over the phone. "I've got a problem."

"What kind of problem?" asked David. "Maybe I can help."

"Well, I was going to open a shoe store — a discount athletic shoe outlet in a building across from ·the Bellevue Mall. I bought 1500 pairs of shoes as inventory, which I have stored in my warehouse. Unfortunately, new owners bought the building before I could sign the lease, and I lost the space. So now I've got to unload the shoes."

"What brands?"

"Mostly knock-offs, but good-quality stuff, all sizes, men's and women's both. I'm only asking six dollars a pair."

David multiplied quickly in his head; that would come to a total of $9000, much too big an investment in off brand shoes.

"Six is too rich for me. I could give you a third of that."

The man said nothing for a minute, then: "Okay, I can come down to five dollars a pair."

This time David paused. "Thirty-five hundred for the lot is as high as I can go."

"No way I can let them go for that little. These are good shoes! You won't have any trouble getting rid of them."

"I appreciate your situation, but I just can't invest that much money in this kind of a deal — the risk is too great." David explained. He found that many of the people who called him didn't understand how his end of the operation worked. They assumed that he had a ready market for their merchandise, that he always came out fine while profiting from their misfortune. The reality was that he gambled with every deal he made and usually had to work the phones hard to move whatever he had bought. Getting stuck with an item and losing his money were very real hazards of the job.

David looked at the clock — a little after four on Friday afternoon. "My offer is good until Sunday at noon. I've

got another deal in the works for Monday, so after Sunday I won't have the capital to help you out. Let me know."

David hung up the phone, switching on his answering machine as he did so. He'd had enough wheeling and dealing for one day. Lately he found that the constant haggling on both the buying and selling ends — was wearing him down, sapping his vitality. David had found that the best cure for mental fatigue was physical exercise. Grabbing his car keys and duffle bag, he headed out to the Westside Gym, ready to work up a sweat.

On the way, he decided to stop by the Heart and Mind Health Food Store, something he did quite often lately. He always had a good reason — today he was going to buy some more protein powder. But, in his heart, he knew he was hoping to bump into Rachel while he was there and once again seeing The Black in the flesh.

Noon on Sunday found Rachel sitting at the Lake Washington Café, an exclusive eatery perched on stilts above its namesake lake, giving diners a to-die-for view. She had agreed to meet Michael for Sunday brunch, a decision she was beginning to question as she waited for him at a small corner table.

"Rachel." Suddenly he was there, impeccably dressed as usual, taking her hand and kissing her on the cheek. "You look great." He sat down opposite her and looked into her eyes. "I'm so glad you agreed to meet me. I've been wanting to see you for a long time."

Rachel laughed. "That's nice of you to say — especially since the last time you saw me, I was fleeing down the aisle of the church."

Michael smiled easily. "Yes, I can still see that becoming bow on the rear of your wedding gown bouncing on your retreating backside. But I don't want to talk about that."

The waiter appeared and handed them menus, giving Rachel a chance to break away from Michael's intent gaze. What a guy, thought Rachel. She had first met him when her parents had built a new home several years ago. He owned the lumberyard that supplied all the lumber for the construction, and he'd often visited the building site to make sure his customers were happy. The day the roof trusses arrived, Rachel had been there, adding a helping hand to the construction crew. Michael had been so impressed that he asked her out on the spot and that had led to a four-year relationship.

During that time, Michael asked Rachel several times to marry him, and finally she had agreed. But she had always harbored misgivings, worrying that she didn't really love him. She had felt affection, respect, admiration but not excitement, never that electric connection of mind and spirit and body.

Michael was staid, stable, predictable — just what she needed, according to her father, Walter. Walter had been instrumental in influencing Rachel's decision to marry Michael, pointing out that Rachel had already passed her thirtieth birthday, and Michael was not only a good guy, but a rich one as well. Rachel knew that her father had

only wanted the best for her, and he was convinced that Michael was it.

At the last minute, however, as Rachel stood at the altar, she had looked first at Walter and then at Michael. With tears streaming down her face, she had shaken her head. "I'm sorry, Michael. To marry you would be unfair. Please, forgive me."

She had run back down the aisle and out into the street, hopping into a waiting limo which had taken her home. She heard later that Michael, gentleman that he was, had apologized to the shocked and teary-eyed guests and insisted that everyone go over to the Hyatt Regency where he had a banquet room reserved for the reception. "I've got a lot of good food and champagne waiting for us over there," he had said. "We might as well go and enjoy it." Evidently it had been quite a party. With the help of one of Rachel's bridesmaid's, Anita, Michael had managed to overcome his disappointment. The two had eloped six months later, but the marriage had disintegrated into disappointment and divorce within a year.

Michael and Rachel spent the next hour and a half enjoying a leisurely brunch, catching up on each other's lives, keeping the conversation light. Finally, Rachel broached the subject she knew had brought them there.

"I'm sorry about you and Anita," said Rachel.

"Oh? And would you be referring to the marriage or the divorce?" asked Michael wryly.

"Well, both, I guess. I always thought she had a thing for you, so I wasn't surprised when she stepped in to take my place."

"Not that she ever could," said Michael, turning serious. "I haven't found anyone that makes me feel the way you do."

"And just how do I make you feel?" asked Rachel, genuinely wanting to know.

"Alive. All tingly. Happy. Optimistic. I don't know, there's just something about you that attracts me. Call it chemistry." He looked at her soberly. "But you don't get that same feeling from me, do you."

She shook her head. "No, I don't, and I can't understand why. It seems odd that such strong chemistry should only flow one way. God knows I certainly wanted to feel that way — that's why I agreed to marry you."

Michael sat back, resigned. "Well, I'm not surprised, but I thought it was worth a shot." Suddenly, he leaned forward in his chair, locking her eyes into his. "Rachel, have you ever experienced that feeling of overwhelming passion with anyone? Maybe it's just not going to happen that way for you."

Rachel turned her gaze out the window, looking down on the lake where a regatta painted the water with dozens of white triangles. But she barely noticed the picturesque scene, her thoughts instead on the man she had met briefly at the health food store.

"Yes, I know that feeling at least I think I do." She looked down at her hands, suddenly self-conscious and unsure of herself, embarrassed that she was thinking of a man with whom she had spent such a short time. How could she honestly say she had felt an irresistible attraction to him when she didn't really know him? "What I mean to say is I understand what you're talking about being consumed by an attraction that shuts everything else out. And I also know that, even if I never find the man who makes me feel that way, I'm never going to settle for less."

David cruised across Lake Washington on the Evergreen Point Bridge as he headed home from Bellevue. Rarely was traffic ever this light on the bridge; as one of only two bridges that connected the city of Seattle with its increasingly populated east side, the Evergreen Point Bridge usually looked more like a parking lot than a highway. However, being that it was Sunday afternoon, the commuters were all at home and cars breezed along at a brisk sixty miles an hour.

David had spent the morning at a warehouse checking out several hundred athletic shoes. The man who had called on Friday afternoon had decided he could live with David's offer after all and they had met at the warehouse to verify the inventory and work out the details. Now, returning home, David didn't need to take the bridge; since he lived south of Seattle, he could have driven around the south side of the lake, avoiding the bridges altogether. But it was a beautiful day and David was feeling good after closing the deal. A drive across the lake had sounded like a good idea.

As he neared the western shore of the lake, he looked down at his gas gauge, which showed the red arrow pointing to "E." Quickly, he moved over to the right and exited at the first offramp off the bridge knowing it would

funnel him into the U District, so named for the University of Washington and its denizens. He came to a stop at the red light that greeted him at the bottom of the offramp. As he sat there, he noticed a disabled car on the cross street. A green Jaguar sat on the shoulder of the road he was about to turn onto, its left rear tire sitting flat on the pavement. Next to the car stood a woman with long black hair, her attention fixed on the flattened tire.

David's stomach dropped. Could it be? As soon as the light flashed green, he turned right onto the street and pulled up behind the Jag. The woman looked up at him. It was The Black.

When Rachel left her meeting with Michael to drive home, she decided — and she didn't quite know why — that she would take the Evergreen Point Bridge, an option she didn't often choose. She had nearly made it across when she was startled by a loud bang and immediately felt a bumpety thump, thump, thump.

Oh, no, she thought, I've blown a tire.

She pulled over as quickly as she could, luckily making it to the first offramp. Once stopped, she got out to inspect the damage.

Hardly the helpless type, Rachel had made a career of doing things that woman generally didn't do. Changing a tire was a piece of cake to her — except she knew she didn't have a jack. She had lent hers to her friend June a few days before and hadn't gotten it back — which meant she now needed to commandeer another to change her tire.

As she was looking down at the tire in question, she heard a car pull up. She hated having to rely on a stranger to rescue her; still she headed toward the car gratefully.

"Hi," she started out. "Looks like I've got a flat tire. I just need a jack. Do you...? She stopped abruptly, staring at the man who had stopped to help her. My God, she thought. It's him!

Rachel and David came together, silently looking into each other's eyes. Neither spoke for a few moments. Finally, David said, "Yes, I've got a jack. I'll get it for you." It took him several seconds to tear himself away from Rachel's gaze and go back to the trunk of his car for the jack.

He returned to Rachel who held out her hand.
"Thanks. I can take it from here," she said.
David withdrew the jack. "I'm sorry. No one uses this jack but me." He smiled at her openly. "I'm afraid you're going to have to let met change the tire."

"I can do it myself," Rachel protested.
"I'm sure you can," replied David. He gave Rachel an appraising look, taking in the finely tailored peach-colored suit she was wearing that accentuated her shapely figure and dark coloring. "But would you please give me the pleasure of doing it for you?"

Rachel smiled and nodded, and David felt every inch of his body come alive.

It took him almost ten minutes to complete the task. "That should do it," he said, standing up. He walked back to his car, where he wrapped up the jack and stowed it away. Closing the trunk, he turned to find Rachel standing close to him. Without any trace of hesitation or self-consciousness, she reached for his hand and wordlessly looked up into his eyes.

Captivated, David stared back, losing himself in the depths of her huge brown eyes. He felt as though he were looking into her innermost self, reading her most intimate thoughts. "Are you the one?" she seemed to be asking. "Are you The Lion I've been searching for all my life?" Finally, she said simply, "Thank you."

David grasped her other hand. "Do you believe in destiny?" he asked, his eyes searching hers.

Slowly, Rachel nodded. "Yes, I do."

"Rachel, I believe you are my destiny am yours.

His words hung in the air for what seemed an eternity and then, suddenly, their bodies came together, their lips found each other, and they stood entwined in-a powerful yet tender embrace, oblivious to the traffic rushing past them. It was several minutes until the horn honking and applause of passing motorists and pedestrians, some of whom had stopped to watch, penetrated their consciousness.

David opened his eyes and found that he had lifted Rachel several inches off the ground. He set her down gently and reluctantly pulled away.

"I'm so glad I finally found you," he told her, stroking her long black hair. "I was afraid I would never see you again."

She looked at him with wonder. "I felt exactly the same way. I She stopped and looked around, once again aware of where they were. "I have so much to tell you, but not here, not now." She smiled up at him. "We have all the time in the world."

"The rest of our lives, said David, and he kissed her again to the delight of the crowd.

CHAPTER 7

Before David sent Rachel on her way that Sunday afternoon, he made sure he had her phone number and promised to call her soon. Then, lightheaded with exhilaration, he got back on the freeway, completely forgetting about the empty gas tank that had prompted his exit in the first place. Luckily, just as his car started to sputter and cough, he spotted an offramp and was able to coast down into the self-serve station that stood at the bottom.

Once home, David took a long, hot shower, dressed in clean sweats, and whipped up a refreshing fruit smoothie. Then, making himself comfortable in his favorite chair, he dialed Rachel's number.

"Hello?" came Rachel's voice across the line, sounding a bit breathless and very sexy.

"It's me. David."

Her laugh sounded warm, spontaneous, inviting. "Already?" she asked, obviously amused.

"I said soon, and this was as soon as I could call. You will find that you can count on me to do what I say.

"I'm sure I'll learn all sorts of wonderful things about you. At least I hope so."

Encouraged, David took a deep breath and plunged ahead. "I want to see you as soon as possible." When Rachel didn't reply right away, he continued, "I don't mean to rush you, and it's not that I'm desperate for company. It's just that. . . " He paused, trying to find the words that would convey the intensity of his belief and longing. "I wasn't being melodramatic today when I talked about our destiny. I've known for a long time that I was waiting for someone special, someone who was meant to be with me. I believe that person is you, and now that I've found you, I don't want to wait anymore."

"I know," said Rachel, quietly. "I mean, I understand about the waiting. But I didn't know I was waiting for a particular person. I just thought I was never going to find anyone who could fulfill my expectations. But. . . since I met you. . ." Her voice trailed off uncertainly, then she laughed again, lightening the moment. "Are you sure you're the one?"

"I'm positive, and I am going to prove it to you. Are you free tomorrow night? Let me take you out to a romantic dinner. I know a great place it has fine food, a spectacular view, and it's cozy and dark. An intimate dinner there would be a great way to begin our lives together."

Rachel thought for a moment. "Sounds great — but I think for our first date I'd like something a little more low key. How about a quiet dinner at my house? That way we can talk, really get to know each other — see if what you think is true."

A beginning even better than I'd hoped for, thought David. Her invitation only served to reinforce his conviction. "You're on. I can't wait."

The next day Rachel went to work as usual, but her thoughts strayed from her tasks all day long, as though her mind had a life of its own. She found herself giggling for no reason, and even the chronic complaints she had to handle couldn't get her down. Still, she felt an undercurrent of apprehension: What had she gotten herself into? A complete stranger, someone who seemed to be obsessed with her, was coming over to her house tonight. They would be alone. She knew nothing about him, not even his last name. She could be letting herself in for not just an unpleasant evening, but a potentially dangerous one.

She reflected on what little she knew about him: how he had taken her slap and unjust accusation without anger; how he had sought her out to apologize again the next day; how he had stopped to help her on the side of the road. No, her gut feeling told her that this was a good guy; now it was time to find out if he was THE guy her Lion.

He certainly looked the part. His physique was superb, muscular and well-proportioned. And though he must be at least six feet tall, he moved with cat-like grace, a quiet confidence in his stride. His features were not classically

handsome, but certainly very attractive in a rugged, masculine way. And that mane of hair — thick, tawny, and not quite to his shoulders had brought the image of a lion to her mind when they had first met.

Rachel's vision of David vanished with a friendly rap on her door. She looked up to see June's stiffly permed head peaking inside the doorway.

"June! Get in here!" Rachel said.

"What did I do?" asked June pretending to be worried.

"You forgot to return my jack. And because of that, my whole life is about to change." Rachel told June all about David, their first meeting at the health food store, the flat tire, the kiss. June smiled broadly as she listened.

"Good on you, girl. It's about time. Now, I have something to tell you, or have you heard already?"

"Heard what?"

June lowered her voice dramatically to deliver her bit of juicy gossip.

"Bill Wick's been canned."

"What? How do you know?"

"Well, I heard from Miko who heard from Terri — you know, that temp who's been filling in as Bill's secretary? — that he's been sent down to California for his health, given an indefinite leave of absence. I'll lay two-tone odds that he's at Betty Ford right now, readjusting his pharmaceutically enhanced personality."

"How do you know he's not coming back?"

"Because Terri says that Evan has spent the last two days going through all the papers in Bill's office. And she found Bill's business cards dumped in the wastepaper basket.' Here it comes, thought Rachel. Ken was right. "Well, some people think the News is going down," she said to June.

"Yep, and I'm one of them. You better start looking for another job, kiddo."

"What about you?" asked Rachel. "What will you and Howard do?"

"Oh, it's time for us to retire, anyway," replied June blithely. "We'll probably sell our house and just live in the motor home. We don't need much money. We've always just worked at the paper for the fun of it."

With a wave, June moved on down the hall. Rachel's good mood began to wane, and then rose again. Who knows? If she was going to lose her job, maybe meeting David right now wasn't just coincidence, but providence. After all, if she were unemployed, she'd be available — and ready — to do anything.

Get a grip, she told herself. You barely know the guy. Let's take things one at a time.

At ten minutes to eight, David climbed into the BMW, carefully setting a dozen persimmon-hued roses and a bottle of expensive champagne on the passenger's seat beside him. He wore a tuxedo, one he had bought several years ago for a cousin's wedding and had rarely worn since.

He had memorized the directions to Rachel's, which turned out to be only a few miles from where he lived — making it all the more astonishing that they had bumped into each other again so far from home and on a road neither of them ever used.

Rachel's small, neat, Cape-Cod-grey house sat on a large lot attractively landscaped with native shrubs and bright flowers. David parked his car in her driveway, and, with roses and champagne in hand, he walked up the brick walkway to her door.

Before he had a chance to knock, Rachel swung open the door. She wore a creamy, clingy sweater with matching skirt, an outfit that provided a striking contrast to her sun-tanned skin and dark hair.

"Come on in," she said and stepped back to let him enter.

David walked into the front room, feeling at home at once. It was furnished in eclectic elegance — well-worn antiques found themselves sharing space with more modern pieces. A boldly striped sofa cozied up to a chintz-covered love seat. But all the furnishings shared classic lines and muted colors that conveyed a sense of good taste and homey comfort.

"I like your house," said David, turning to look at Rachel. "It fits you well."

For the next few moments, he allowed himself the pleasure of just looking at her, drinking her in, little by little. He started with the hair — so black and with a healthy shine that reminded him of burnished onyx. Then the soulful eyes, set off by the high, wide cheekbones; the full lips, slightly parted into a knowing smile; the firm chin, lifted a bit as if in anticipation. His eyes moved down to the slender shoulders which set off the full and nicely shaped breasts, the narrow waist and flat stomach, the legs that tapered perfectly to slim ankles. "You are beautiful."

Rachel blushed. "Are those for me?" she asked, indicating the roses.

"They are, but you put them to shame." He handed them to her and lifted the champagne bottle. "1 don't usually drink very much, but tonight I wanted to celebrate.

Rachel gave him a radiant smile. "Sit down and make yourself comfortable. I'll get the champagne flutes."

As David waited, he looked around the room, eager to know more about the woman he thought of as The Black. The first thing he noticed were the books, all of them hardbound and neatly arranged on mahogany shelves that completely covered one wall of the room. He browsed some of the titles, impressed by the variety of the interests they reflected. Against another wall he noticed a beautiful tiger-oak sideboard.

On it, next to an immense jade plant, sat two pictures — one of an elderly women and the other of a man and a woman, arm in arm. Not wanting to be caught snooping, he moved to the couch, sinking down into its comfy cushions, and was immediately joined by a small, white cat with distinctive black markings. She turned her green eyes on him with interest for a few moments. Then, daintily, she climbed onto his lap.

"Oh, do you like cats?" asked Rachel, returning to the room with the glasses. "Just shoo her away if you don't."
"She's fine," said David. "I take it as a good sign that she seems to like me."

Rachel set two gold-rimmed champagne glasses on the butler's table and, wrapping a towel around the champagne bottle, handed it to David to uncork. Placing Kido on the arm of the couch, David took the bottle and eased the cork out with a soft pop. Fizzling vapors escaped from the dark green neck but none of the wine bubbled out. After filling the glasses, David handed one to Rachel and lifted his own.

"To the woman I have seen only in my dreams, until now. To the person I hope to bring happiness — tonight, tomorrow, and forever. To the one and only Black."

He leaned forward to clink Rachel's glass with his, but Rachel didn't move to meet him. Instead, an odd expression crossed her face, one of delighted disbelief.

"What is it?" asked David.

"How did you know?"

"That you are the woman for me? Well, that's a long story I hope to have the opportunity to tell you."

"No," said Rachel, a becoming flush rising on her cheekbones. "Not that. How did you know my name?"

David looked at her, not understanding. He knew only that her name was Rachel because she had told him so.

"Black," explained Rachel, seeing his confusion. "My last name is Black. But I never told you."

A chill went down David's spine. Then he smiled at Rachel and leaned forward to give her a slow, soft, sensuous kiss.

"I didn't know your name. I just knew you were the woman I had been searching for, my Black Beauty."

For David and Rachel, the evening was one of pure enchantment.

They spent the first hour on the couch, sipping champagne and painting the first broad strokes of the stories of their lives. Rachel learned that David, who had been abandoned by his father and abused by a drug addicted mother, had been raised in a foster home by good people whom he regarded as his parents. Rachel talked about her more typical childhood, an only child of loving parents Walter and Lydia, whose picture adorned the sideboard. They now lived out toward the coast where Lydia owned a gift shop. They hardly needed the income, however, since Walter had won a $20 million state lottery a couple of years before.

Eventually they moved into the kitchen, where Rachel prepared the main course while David chopped vegetables. Working together companionably, they talked some more, discovering a common thread in their lives. Given his upbringing, David had learned to be independent and self-sufficient early on. Although he always tried to treat others with respect and courtesy, he rarely opened up to people and he had few friends, partly because he did not want to come to rely on anyone else. Rachel, too, was independent by nature. She didn't have many girlfriends, and she had often taken on jobs that were unusual for a woman, which fueled her natural tendency to be a bit of a loner.

In the glow of muted candlelight, as they dined on poached salmon, stir-fried vegetables, and pine nut and brown rice pilaf, the conversation ebbed. They ate slowly and said little, instead enjoying the satisfying sensation of a fine meal shared with excellent company. At one point, David reached out his hand and Rachel placed hers within its tender grasp; later on, Rachel slipped off a shoe and let her foot gently caress David's calf under the table. The meal evolved into an erotic, sensual, enjoyable experience unlike any either had ever known.

Finally, they moved back into the living room but this time they pushed the butler's table away from the couch and settled side by side on the floor atop a cushy sheepskin rug. They sat close together, sipping decaffeinated coffee laced with Bailey's Irish Creme. The electricity between them was palpable; yet both Rachel and David seemed more interested in exploring their extraordinary connection rather than succumbing to the immediate gratification of carnal desire. While sex was tempting, and inevitable, they had come to some unspoken agreement to go slowly, to nurture those elements of their relationship that went beyond physical attraction. Both understood that they had found something rare and wonderful, and they were content to let it proceed at its own pace.

It wasn't until the antique grandfather's clock that stood in the corner of the living room struck one o'clock that David took notice of the time.

"I'm sorry, I've stayed too long. I'd better go. I know you've got work tomorrow."

He traced the line of her jaw with his finger, and then reluctantly stood up, pulling Rachel with him.

"Yeah, well, it's not like I'm going to have that job for much longer," said Rachel. She let her body be drawn to David's, thinking how nicely they fit.

David looked lovingly into her eyes. "Whatever happens to you, know that you can count on me to help you in any way I can." And then, afraid that he saw apprehension in Rachel's eyes, he quickly said, "Don't worry. I won't smother you. I love your independent nature and wouldn't change that for the world. I just want to do whatever I can to make you happy."

Rachel lowered her eyes and smiled, though David couldn't see it. Can this guy be for real? she thought. She looked up at David and asked, "Do you mean that, regardless of wherever our relationship takes us, whether we become lovers or not, you still want the best for me?" What a loaded question to ask a man!

David didn't waver. "To know you and to love you are one for me. I want whatever you want; but I have no doubt that you and I are destined to be together."

Rachel walked David to his car where he drew her to him in his strong embrace.

"I already love you more than you can ever know," he whispered into her hair. "Don't be afraid. My love is unconditional. No matter how you feel about me, I will always be your friend and champion."

As Rachel watched him drive away, she was overwhelmed by a feeling of wonder and elation and fear.

Dear God, if you are toying with me, stop it now! she silently prayed.

When David returned home, he quickly went through his bedtime routine and then picked up the phone. "Hello?"

"Rachel, I just wanted to say goodnight and to thank you for a wonderful time," David said into the receiver. "It was a special evening for me. But I knew it would be — that's why I wore the tux."

Rachel giggled. "You were wearing a tux? I don't think I even noticed. All I remember is looking into your deep blue eyes all night."

A grin appeared on David's face. Is it possible that she's as swept away as I am? he wondered. "I'll take that as a compliment," he said. "And I was so enthralled I forgot to ask you when I can see you again."

'Not tomorrow night I've got a meeting at the library.'

"The library?' David repeated, inquiringly.

"I do some volunteer work there with the kids. Tomorrow night some of the staff and volunteers are getting together to plan the children's activities for the fall. I really wouldn't feel right missing it just because I had a better offer."

"No, I wouldn't want you to do that," agreed David, though a bit disappointed. "How about Wednesday?"

"Not soon enough for me, but I'll take it. Sleep well."

David put the phone back in the cradle and turned out the lights. That Rachel did volunteer work, and took her commitment seriously, gave him one more thing to love about her. He had always felt that donating his time and talents to community projects was worthwhile and had done so on a number of occasions. He often conducted classes on exercise and nutrition for seniors and had spent

several summers working with kids at a Christian summer camp. As he lay down to go to sleep, a warm glow engulfed him. She is perfect, he thought to himself. She is the one.

Five minutes later, just as he was drifting off, the phone rang. Thinking it was Rachel, he picked it up and said, "I was just falling asleep dreaming about you."

"Well, that must have been one hell of a nightmare," came a man's raspy voice across the line.

David sat up quickly. "Who is this?" he demanded. A burst of static briefly interrupted the response.

"...recognize your old friend Jack's voice?" came the laughing answer.

"Jack!" David cried, fully awake now. "How the hell are you? Where the hell are you?"

Before Jack could answer, another jolt of heavy static crackled across the line, cutting off communication for several seconds.

"You there?" David heard Jack's voice asking him.

"Yeah, I can hear you," he replied, but no sooner did he get the words out of his mouth than the interference erupted again, this time even louder than before. David held the receiver away from his ear as he patiently waited for the line to clear.

"...damnit. . . no good...junk..." David could hear snippets of Jack's voice between bursts of static, and he knew his friend was using some of his most colorful language to urge the phone to work. David wondered if Jack was calling from somewhere deep in the heart of Africa, his last known destination, where he had hoped to seek his fortune exporting native birds.

Finally, the interference cleared, and Jack's voice came down the line.

"David, I'm gonna have to get back..." Static once again obliterated whatever else he said, and the line went dead.

David returned the receiver to its cradle and thought about Jack, who was one of his oldest friends. They had met several years ago when Jack owned a couple of pet stores in the Seattle area and David had bought a beautiful blue Macaw parrot from him. They got to talking, and when Jack mentioned that he planned to remodel his stores, David, who knew the construction trade, offered his services. Jack eventually sold his stores and decided to start his own business exporting exotic birds. As far as David knew, he'd spent the last several months down in Africa hoping to stock up on his inventory. David missed Jack's company and hoped he had called to say was returning to the States.

David fell back onto his pillow, his mind filled with memories of the good times he and Jack had shared. But soon his thoughts drifted back to what he fantasized about every night when he went to bed — The Black. Tonight, however, was different.

Tonight, the fantasy had become a reality.

CHAPTER 8

To David, waiting another two days to see Rachel seemed an eternity. To pass the time, he threw himself into his work, placing calls from Hawaii to Maine, from Texas to Ottawa, trying to find a home for the 1500 pairs of unwanted athletic shoes. His diligence paid off; an outlet store in Calgary agreed to buy them at $6.50 Canadian a pair, netting David a nice profit.

That accomplished, David surveyed the mess he called his office, which in most homes would be a dining room. Although he tried to keep his operation neatly organized, sometimes things got out of hand. Now he saw papers, price sheets, and other paraphernalia teetering in sloppy piles. Phone books lay on the dining room table, the coffee table, the kitchen bar. Coffee cups, several with congealing liquid still inside, sat perched in odd places around the condo. Junk mail and catalogs occupied every available corner. It was time to clean house.

David didn't mind; he felt an energy and enthusiasm he had never known. He revved his engine with a protein drink and then went to work. An hour passed in industrious organization, his mind oblivious to the tediousness of his task, for it was filled with the image of the wonderful woman who had finally materialized in his life.

The shrill peal of the phone pierced his thoughts, startling him.

"Trans Pacific Sales. "

"David, it's Dick," came the smooth, professional voice out of the receiver. "Are you busy?"

David had met Dick Sloane three or four years earlier at an auction when David was fairly new to the liquidating business. The two had hit it off, and over the years they had worked together on several business deals. Dick also had hired David on occasion to act as what he called Insurance" — for those times he wasn't too sure about the kind of people he would be dealing with and he wanted some extra muscle to back him up.

David sat down in his swivel chair and put his feet up on the now nearly bare desk. "Just doing some housecleaning. How about yourself. Making any money?"

"Well, funny you should ask. I may have a good deal coming up. But something tells me it would be comforting to have you along for the ride." He paused, and David could hear the sharp intake of breath that comes from a quick drag on a cigarette. "How would you like to go to Vegas?"

"Hot down there this time of year, but I'm game. What do you have?"

"A fax just came through from a guy I've done business with down there. He says he needs to move 3500 pairs of Levi's. Thirty-five grand — cash — takes all. I've never met this guy face to face; we've completed all our deals over the phone. Something tells me he's shifty; he hasn't screwed me yet, but I've heard a few things.

I'd like to have you along to make sure everything stays on the up and up."

"When?"

"Monday morning there's an Alaska Airlines flight out at seven-thirty. If it's okay with you, I'll book two seats. We should be able to come back Tuesday night,

Wednesday at the latest."

"Okay, sign me up."

After working out a few other details, Dick rang off. David went back to his cleaning, thinking about what he had just agreed to. Perhaps he should have asked a few more questions; after all, he could be walking into a dangerous situation. But the high he still felt from his evening with Rachel had dulled his ordinarily wary nature. He felt good all over — as though now that he had found The Black, nothing could go wrong. He was soon to find out otherwise.

Early Wednesday morning, David called Rachel at work and arranged to be at her house at seven, with dinner in hand. On the way over to her house, he stopped off at Koto's, a Japanese restaurant he frequented. Since Rachel was a quasi-vegetarian who ate only fish and shellfish, he wanted to put together a delicious meal that suited her diet. He selected several items from the sushi bar, along with miso soup, skewered shrimp, sticky rice, pickled vegetables, and, of course, green tea.

As he pulled up to Rachel's house, he could see her through the living room window, rushing around to tidy things up before he arrived. He took his time getting from the car to the front door. Once again, she opened it before he could knock.

"Hello," she said, almost shyly.

"Hello." As David moved forward to come in, Rachel didn't give way at once, but instead held her ground, reaching up on her tiptoes to give him a welcoming kiss. Then she stood back, but only a little, so that their bodies brushed as he walked into the house.

"You can just keep going into the kitchen," she told him, following him in. "Shall we eat while everything's still warm?"

David set the packages of food on the kitchen counter, and turned to look at the table, already set with fine china and chopsticks. A trio of lavender orchids peeked out of a bud vase.

He turned to look at her. "The table is beautiful; you are beautiful." And then he said mischievously, "You worked all day, your house is clean and tidy, and you look as though you haven't lifted a finger. You must be one of those people who is naturally neat and organized."

Rachel let out a whoop of laughter and then covered her mouth. "Well, I could lie and say that's true, but the real story is I was running around like crazy trying to get everything done before you got here. And, no, I'm not someone who has everything under control all the time — in fact, I never seem to have enough time." She gave him an impish grin. "But I am trying to make a good impression.

David laughed and put his arms around her. "Beautiful and honest too. How lucky can a guy get?"

Dinner was relaxed as they each unraveled a little bit more about themselves. Rachel talked about the News and how badly things were going.

"I guess I won't be so upset if it goes belly-up," she admitted, slowly sucking a shrimp off its skewer. "Maybe it will force me to pursue my real passion."

David, momentarily mesmerized by the sensuous way in which Rachel was eating her shrimp, blinked and asked, "And that is?"

"Well... apparel design. Actually, what I love to do is create a piece from beginning to end. That means I design it, construct a pattern, select the fabric, and then sew the garment."

David was impressed. "You can do all that?" Suddenly, he noticed what she was wearing: a calf-length shift that exposed most of her tanned shoulders, tailored to fit her curves, made from a fabric with hues of blue in a Polynesian motif. A slit ran up one side, revealing part of her thigh. "Did you make what you're wearing tonight? It's very attractive.

Rachel nodded self-consciously. "I almost didn't wear it, afraid it was too..." she stopped, embarrassed now.

"It's perfect. You look great in it."

David told her about the liquidating business and how it wasn't a job he particularly enjoyed.

"To really do well in this business, you have to be cutthroat. Always try to beat the other guy down, get the best price from both buyer and seller. If you're good, you can make a lot of money. But I don't have that killer instinct like the real movers do. And I often end up feeling sorry for people who have to sell off their stuff."

"Why do you stay in it?" asked Rachel.

David deftly picked up a piece of California roll with his chopsticks and dipped it into the pasty-green wasabi.

"It gives me a lot of freedom. I can pretty much set my own hours. And since I compete in body-building events a couple of times a year, I need the time and a flexible schedule to maintain my workout regimen."

"So that's why your body is so gorgeous," remarked Rachel, openly admiring the muscles that rippled beneath the surface of his knit shirt.

For dessert, they moved into the living room. Rachel lit some candles and popped a mellow jazz CD into the player. Then she brought out a bowl of fresh strawberries, flanked by smaller bowls of sour cream and brown sugar.

David looked at her inquiringly. "Is this some kind of ritual?" he asked.
"No, silly, it's just dessert. Here." She selected a perfect, bright-red berry and, holding it by its stem, she dipped it first into the cream and then into the sugar. "Open up and take a bite."
David did as he was told. His eyes crinkled, revealing his pleasure. "Mmmmmm. That's good."

Rachel picked out another large strawberry and repeated the process; this time, however, she put it to her lips and slowly, seductively, she licked the creamy sugar off the berry.

David watched, enrapt. Their eyes connected, and the undeniable sexual yearning between them suddenly filled the air. Rachel didn't finish the strawberry; instead, she put it down on her napkin and then looked back at David. In an instant, he had pulled her close to him, his lips coming down insistently on hers.

They spent the next several minutes engulfed by their passion, letting the fire they had lit grow until it blazed nearly out of control. Each felt the white-hot intensity that comes with that first erotic encounter, the sweet surrender to irresistible desire that overwhelms the senses. They had nearly reached the point of no return when David drew back, breathing hard.

"Rachel," he panted. He took a minute to regain his composure and slow his racing heart. "There's nothing I want more than to be close to you, to lie naked next to you, to make love to you." He stopped, waiting for the words to come that would express just how he felt.

"But I want it to be at the right time, to be a deliberate act, not just simply giving in to the heat of the moment. I... I'd like to wait."

He saw her look of incredulity and laughed in spite of himself. "I know. I surprise even myself." He took her hand and raised to his lips. "You still don't know how special you are to me. I want everything to be perfect."

Rachel stared at him for a moment, and then leaned back against the cushions on the couch.

"I'll say one thing for you — you sure are different," she sighed, but she said it with a smile. "Why don't I make some coffee?" She picked up the strawberries, giving David a sideways glance. "And no more of these!"

Later, as they sat sipping coffee at the kitchen table, David asked, "Are you free this weekend? I'd love to take you for a drive, maybe go over to Bainbridge Island, do some walking on the beach."

"Oh, I can't. Friday morning I'm taking off with Gran to go up to her cabin on Rimrock Lake and I won't be back until Monday afternoon." When she saw the disappointment in David's eyes, she added, "We've had it planned for weeks. I couldn't possibly cancel now."

"No, of course not. Is that her picture on your sideboard, next to your parents?"

"Yes. She's really a sweetie. I lived with her for a while when my parents moved to the coast. We go on a little outing like this every so often and having a great time." Rachel poured herself another cup of coffee, warming up David's at the same time. "I should be home around four on Monday. Maybe we could see each other that night."

"I'd love to, but I'll be in Las Vegas." David explained his business trip with Dick Sloane, giving her all of the details, even though he suspected she might not like the arrangement. He was determined to keep this relationship completely open and honest.

"Gee, David, that sounds dangerous. Your friend is going to meet some guy he thinks is a crook while carrying $35,000 in cash? Sounds like a setup to me." Her worry and concern were evident, and David felt his heart ache. "Can't you give him a money order or travelers' checks?"

"I guess this guy was very specific about the cash — but that's not unusual in this business. Sometimes people need money right now — and they can't afford to have it go through any banking institutions, especially when the amount is that large."

"I see." Rachel looked down into her coffee. "Will you be taking a gun?" she asked quietly.

"No, I don't do things that way. I rely on my quickness, my strength and fitness, and my intuitive abilities. I've also been trained in the martial arts. I'll admit, there have been a few some rough spots, but I've also learned a lot. I rarely get myself into a situation I can't handle. Actually, what I really do is keep things from going wrong, head off the trouble before it ever surfaces."

"Oh, David, you could get beat up, shot, killed... her voice trailed off miserably, and when she looked up at him, tears spilled down her lovely face. "I knew this was too good to be true."

"Rachel, Rachel," crooned David softly, and he pushed his chair over next to hers. Tenderly he took her in his arms, resting her face against his shoulder, smoothing her hair with his hand. "Remember, I have been waiting for you for a long, long time. I am not going to do anything that will keep us from spending the rest of our lives together."

"If you get killed in Vegas, tonight would be the rest of your life," she pointed out.

David had to laugh. "You've got me there." He reached down and lifted her chin, so he could look into her moist dark eyes. "Just remember I love you. Nothing can keep me from you, ever. I promise."

CHAPTER 9

David met Dick Sloane at the Alaska Airlines ticket counter promptly at six-thirty Monday morning. After checking in, they made their way toward the boarding lounge, visiting a Starbuck's stall along the way to enjoy an expensive latté and over-priced gourmet muffin.

As they stood at the stall drinking their coffee, David watched Dick as he continually looked around the terminal, a nervous habit that was by now familiar to David. David guessed that Dick was in his late forties. Small and wiry, with hair that had already turned a steely gray, Dick reminded David of a wary animal, always on the lookout for stalking prey. As usual, Dick was dressed to the nines, sporting a hand-tailored suit, a silk shirt with French cuffs, and highly polished Italian shoes.

Although they already had their boarding passes, Dick stopped at the counter in the lounge, handing a piece of paper to the uniformed man in attendance. The man gave a little nod and said something to Dick, who then came over and took a seat next to David.

"Now boarding, Alaska Airlines flight #502, nonstop service to Las Vegas," came the melodious voice over the loud speaker.

David started to rise, but Dick put a restraining hand on his arm.

"Let's wait," he suggested. "I'd like to be one of the last people to board.

David sat back down without question. He knew from experience that Dick always had a good reason for whatever he did. Sure enough, after everyone else had boarded, the man at the counter motioned to Dick and David.

"Come on," said Dick, heading over to the counter. David followed, and they were both given a new boarding pass, one which allowed them to sit in first class.

Once they settled in, David turned to Dick with a sly grin. "And how did you manage this?" he asked. "Or do I not want to know?"

"Just a favor someone wanted to do for me. I didn't want to offend them, so I am graciously accepting their hospitality."

Over- a truly delicious breakfast, Dick explained their agenda for the day.

"I've got a rental car waiting at Hertz, a Cad to make us look prosperous. We'll jump into that and head over to a small hotel off the Strip. They know me there and I get big service at little prices."

"Seems like a lot of people owe you favors," observed David.

"Hey, I'm a likable guy. I do nice things for other people all the time," protested Dick. "They're just showing me their appreciation."

For what wasn't the first time, David wondered whether some of Dick's business associates were on the shady side. Some of the deals Dick had scored had seemed too good to be true, and he often needed someone like David around for security reasons. And, after all, this was Vegas; most people who made a living here had some contact with the Mob. But David never felt it was his place to ask. Dick had hired him to do a job; he would do whatever it took to make sure Dick got the deal done and remained in one piece.

After they checked into their room at the Sundowner, Dick made a few calls while David went through a light workout in the hotel's gym. They ate a late lunch in the coffee shop and then headed down the Strip toward the south end of town to meet Dick's contact, a Mr. Blackburn.

The address they had been given belonged to a nameless storefront in a strip mall that had seen better days. Every window was protected by wrought-iron bars, as was the front door. Today this stood open, however, and long strands of plastic beads hung from the top of the doorsill to the ground.

David parked the car in the adjacent lot, locked it, and then followed Dick to the door of the shop. The clink of the dangling baubles announced the two men's arrival as they stepped into the murky gloom of the store, their eyes taking a moment to adjust. Items for sale sat on shelves and tables everywhere, all covered by a heavy layer of dust that suggested they had been abandoned there. Three glassed-in display cases filled with jewelry and

semiprecious stones stood side by side, separating the front of the store from the rear. Behind this counter they could see a lanky, dark-haired man, his back to the entrance, a phone sandwiched between his left shoulder and ear.

"I don't give a damn what they told you," he was saying menacingly into the receiver. "Get the money here by five or I make a phone call." He turned and quickly glanced over his shoulder at Dick and David, a smile flashing across his swarthy face. His tone of voice changed immediately. "Yes, five o'clock would be just fine. And thank you again," he purred into the phone and then placed it back into the cradle.

"Mr. Sloane?" he asked, coming toward Dick. "Ahh, it's good to finally meet you in person." He hurried out from behind the counter, extending a ring-studded hand to Dick.

Dick gave the hand a quick shake. "This is my associate, Mr. Brooks," he said, indicating David.

"Ah, Mr. Brooks, so glad you could be here to help us in our little venture, intoned Mr. Blackburn, giving David a clammy, limp hand to shake. "As I'm sure Mr. Sloane has told you, I am one of the largest and most successful liquidators in Nevada. That's why I get first pick of the deals, and this is a sweet one."

David retrieved his hand and smiled politely at Mr. Blackburn, but the little hairs on the back of his neck were standing at attention. He knew the smell of deception, and its aroma hung heavily in the air.

Dick and Mr. Blackburn discussed the details of the deal. They were to meet with the sellers at 10 A.M. the next day at a warehouse on the east side of town.

"You, of course, have cash?" inquired Mr. Blackburn smoothly, looking from Dick to David.

"We'll have it tomorrow," replied Dick, casually.

"Good. Why don't you meet me here at nine-thirty and we can ride over together?"

Before Dick could answer, David said, "Thanks anyway, but we will be coming straight from a breakfast meeting, so we'll have to meet you there. I'll be driving, so I'll need some directions."

Plainly, Mr. Blackburn didn't like this arrangement; reluctantly he gave David the address and directions, plus a word of advice.

"Don't be late," he warned. "These people are on a tight schedule. If you show up at ten-fifteen, you could lose the deal."

Dick and David assured him they would be on time and then retreated through the brightly colored beads and back into the blazing sunlight.

"Well, what do you think?" asked Dick, once they were back in the car.

"It smells," said David. "That guy has something up his sleeve. I'd bet on it. What do you say we drive over to the warehouse and check the place out right now?"

Ten minutes later David wheeled the car into the huge parking lot that fronted a row of large buildings. The one they wanted housed a flea market that was open in the afternoons and on weekends. First, they drove around the outside, checking out exits; there were only two, the main entrance facing the street and a loading dock in the rear that opened onto a narrow alley. Next, they went inside, heading past the stalls to a cleared area in the rear of the building where, according to Mr. Blackburn, the deal would go down.

On their way back to the hotel, Dick told David to stop at the shopping mall.

"What size Levi's do you wear?" he asked David, as he got out of the car.

"What? Why?"

"Because I'm going to buy a pair of the real thing, so I can use them to compare with the ones we'll see tomorrow. That will help me figure out if what they're offering are counterfeit. I've got more Levi's than I can wear, so I thought I'd buy you a pair."

"You? Wearing Levi's?" asked David. "That, I'd like to see."

"Just tell me your size, wise guy," replied Dick.

David smiled and followed him into the jeans store, where Dick paid cash for a size 31 by 34.

Later that evening, Dick went downstairs to gamble, but David remained in his room. He was tired, and he missed Rachel. He took a relaxing soak in the jet tub, put on a clean T-shirt and underwear, turned on the TV, and lay down on the bed, his head propped up on the pillow.

Moving the phone over onto the bed, he picked up the receiver, and dialed her number. Then he closed his eyes, listening to the rings, anticipating the seductive sound of her voice, picturing her dark eyes, her full lips, the curve of her chin, the "Hello? . . . Hello?" A man's gruff voice leapt from the phone, startling David out of his fantasy. Momentarily disoriented, he wondered whom he had actually called.

"Uh... I . . . I'm calling for Rachel, Rachel Black. Is... I mean... .do I have the right number?"

"It's the right number." The man paused, and David thought to himself, how can that be? Is this her husband? Oh, God, has she been lying to me all along? Before he could decide what to say, the man spoke again, and David could hear a sob in his voice. "I'm sorry. You're too late."

"Too late? What do you mean? Is she out?" David wondered what the hell was going on. Who was this man and why was he so upset?

"No." The man paused, trying to steady his voice. "I'm Rachel's father. Is this... are you a friend of Rachel's?"

More than a friend, thought David, but since he hadn't yet met Rachel's dad, he simply answered, "Yes."

"I'm sorry to have to tell you this." Again, the sound of a sob came across the line. "Rachel is... she's dead. A drunk driver hit and killed her this afternoon as she was driving home from work."

David stared at the phone, and then, as if hit by a bolt of lightning, he shot off the bed, letting out an anguished roar of grief. Then, without thinking, he picked up the nightstand, letting a lamp crash to the floor, and flung it across the room, smashing the piece to bits.

He gazed for a moment at the destruction, and then sank back onto the bed, his hands covering his face.

"Oh, Jesus, please, please hear me. I'll do anything, anything, but, please, don't let this be happening," David prayed. And suddenly he heard a comforting voice in his head saying everything would be okay.

"okay?" The voice wasn't in David's head, but real. It belonged to Dick, who was shaking David's arm and saying, "Hey, sleepyhead, time to get in bed and turn out the lights. Okay?"

David opened his eyes and blinked unbelievingly. His prayer had been answered! He grabbed Dick and gave him a big hug.

"Hey!' laughed Dick, pushing David away. "I'm not that kind of guy!"

"Geez, Dick, you don't know what just happened to me!" David flopped back on the bed and squeezed his eyes shut to blot out the horrible memory. Had it all been just a dream? He looked around the room. The nightstand stood next to the bed, all in one piece, the lamp sitting atop it, intact. But· it had seemed so real, David thought, so vivid. Then, a frightening thought suddenly hit him, and he sat back up quickly. "I'll tell you all about it tomorrow. First, I've gotta make a phone call."

David carefully dialed Rachel's number, and when she answered with a sleepy hello, he breathed a sigh of relief.

"I just called to say, 'Sweet dreams,'" he said softly.

"Take care and I'll talk to you tomorrow."

The next morning, Dick and David got up early and went down to the all-you-can-eat buffet in the casino. Once they had settled at their table, Dick started briefing David.

"I know you know what to do, but let's just go over a couple of things. If I start acting funny, that means something's up, so follow my lead. If I don't like what I see, I'll probably make up some cock-and-bull story and try to get the hell out of there. Things might get hairy but then that's why I brought you along."

David stuffed a big bite of blueberry blintz into his mouth, chewing and swallowing it before he answered. "You think they might have a gun?"

Dick nodded. "It's possible. I want you to be ready for that possibility."

"Well, don't worry about it," he said, using the freshly starched linen napkin to wipe a smear of blueberry from his mouth. "I've been known to disarm a man before he has time to pull the trigger — or have you forgotten our little Spokane escapade?"

A couple of years earlier, Dick had enlisted David's services in helping him recover an outstanding debt. It seemed that a Mr. Bratton had stiffed Dick on a big order and still owed him $11,000. When Dick had tried to collect, however, Mr. Bratton had advised him to drop the matter "if he knew what was good for him."

David had accompanied Dick to Spokane, where they had driven out to Bratton's new, large, luxury home. Before they could knock on the door, Bratton had come out into the front yard, brandishing a gun, threatening to blow their heads off. But he made the fatal mistake of letting David get too close. With catlike quickness, David had taken the gun from Bratton and handed it to Dick.

"I don't like to do business this way," Dick had said, leveling the gun barrel at Bratton, "but you give me no choice. Now, either hand over the cash or something of equal value."

Without his gun Bratton's bravado had crumbled and he had signed over an older silver Rolls Royce that was parked in his garage. Dick and David had returned to Seattle in style; a few days later, when Dick sold the car for $16,000, he had kept $11,000, paid David his fee of $2500, and" sent the remaining $2500 back to Bratton. Knowing that Dick didn't keep any more than what was due him, even though Bratton had tried to cheat him, really impressed David. Ever since that day, he had trusted Dick implicitly.

At five minutes to ten, Dick and David pulled into the lot at the flea market and got out of the car. They first tried the doors at the rear of the building but found them locked. The front entrance was open, however, and they walked into the building, slowly, cautiously. Since the flea market didn't open until noon, the stalls were deserted, the building eerily silent.

They walked to the rear of the building, but saw no sign of Mr. Blackburn nor the rumored Levi's.

"I guess we're early," observed Dick.

No sooner were the words out of his mouth than they heard the sound of a truck pulling up outside. Suddenly, the rear door swung open and two men and a woman strode in. All were very blond and dressed completely in black.

Dick gave David a sideways glance, as if to say, "Watch my back."

"Are you here for the Levi's?" asked one of the men. His English was heavily accented. David guessed that they were either German or Austrian.

"Yeah, I am," replied Dick, and then he added, "You know, that's strange. We tried to come in that door, but it was locked."

The man gave him a cold smile and simply said, "The Levi's are outside in the truck."

"Shouldn't we wait for Mr. Blackburn?" asked Dick, somewhat surprised. "I thought this was his deal."

The woman spoke up. "Mr. Blackburn had an emergency to attend to," she explained in a flat, harsh voice that carried the same accent as her cohort. "He advised us to go ahead without him."

"Please," said the first man, opening the door, "we don't have much time." Dick shot David a wary look and started toward the open door which led out onto the loading dock. David followed, all of his senses poised to pick up the slightest misstep from the Germans. Just as Dick was about to pass through the door, however, one of the men held up his hand, a silent command for Dick to halt.

"You have the money? Thirty-five thousand cash?'"

"I do, Dick assured him smoothly. Again, he showed no evidence of nerves, acting as if they were talking about just a few dollars. "But, not on me, you understand. It's in the safety deposit box at the hotel." He produced a piece of paper. "The hotel manager gave me this receipt as proof to show you."

He handed an official-looking piece of paper to the German and then walked through the door as though he didn't have a care in the world. David, on the other hand, was tense and alert, ready for any sign of violence. Once outside, Dick hopped into the back of a large U-Haul van and surveyed the piles of jeans.

"I'd like a few minutes to look them over," he said amiably to the German, flipping open a pocket calculator.

"The man fixed Dick with a cold stare. "Don't take too long," he ordered. He moved over to the other end of the loading dock, sat down against a wall, and lit a cigarette. From where he sat, he could see only whether anyone came out of the van, but not what went on inside.

Dick motioned to David and whispered, "Help me find a 31 by 34. Hurry!" Both men searched for several minutes, finding all sorts of combinations except the one they wanted.

"I've got one," Dick finally announced triumphantly. "David, quick, toss me your briefcase."

David had been carrying the new pair of Levi's in a black leather briefcase and now he pitched it to Dick. "Forty-three, sixty-nine, eleven," he directed him. Dick dialed the specifics and snapped open the locks. Out fell the Levi's.

David watched as Dick held the store-bought pair up to the Levi's found in the trailer. The differences were evident; the Germans' Levi's were four inches longer and two inches narrower in the waist.

Dick shook his head. "They're counterfeit. Damnit!' He looked at David. "Okay, let me do the talking, and let's just try to get out of here quietly."

Dick and David jumped from the trailer bed onto the loading dock, just as the other man and the woman came out. The man who had been keeping guard stood up, and suddenly the confrontation took on the air of a showdown.

"What's taking so long?" asked the woman. Her features were sharp and symmetrical, and the angry sneer on her face erased any appeal she might have had.

"Just routine," explained Dick. "I wanted to look over the merchandise, and I'm afraid the quality is not up to the standards of the client I'm buying for. However, I think I can still cut a deal. I have a couple of other customers I'm sure will be very interested." He paused as though he were thinking. "I'll tell you what. I'm going to go back to the hotel and contact them. If they give me the go ahead, I have the cash at the hotel, as I said — to close the deal."

He made a show of looking at his watch. "Why don't I call Mr. Blackburn at one o'clock and let him know? We can meet back here later to exchange the cash and goods."

No one said anything for a minute, and then the woman let loose with a string of expletives that would put any sailor to shame. As one of the men tried to placate her, Dick purposefully headed for the door that led inside the building, with David close on his heels. They were just about to close it behind them when the other man noticed their departure.

"Hey!' he yelled and lunged at David, catching hold of the briefcase. David turned, planted a foot on the man's chest, and with a swift kick sent him flying. Then David
slipped inside the door and Dick shut it tight, sliding in the dead bolt to secure it.

"Come on!" he shouted.
They sprinted the length of the building, dashed out the front entrance, and jumped into their car which they had luckily left unlocked. Without a backwards glance, they sped out the lot and down the road.

"Whew!" sighed Dick. "I'm getting too old for this." And then, with a sidelong glance at David, he burst out laughing.
David just smiled and shook his head. "You and me both, boss. You and me both."

CHAPTER 10

Dick and David caught an early afternoon flight out of Vegas; by four, they had landed safely at Sea-Tac airport and parted ways.

The first thing David did was to call Rachel at work.

Expecting to hear Ellen's usual melodic "Good afternoon, Personnel," he was surprised when Rachel herself answered the phone.

"Rachel Black."

David drank in the rich, sultry tones, thirsty for the sound of her voice. "Hello, my beautiful Black," he said.

"David! I'm so glad to hear your voice. Are you still in Vegas?"

"Nope, I'm home well, actually, I'm at the airport. I want to see you as soon as I can. Can I come by your office?"

Rachel laughed. "I've got a better idea. How about meeting me at my place in an hour?"

David glanced at his watch. "With rush-hour traffic, it'll probably take me that long. But what about work?"

"There is no more work," sighed Rachel. "As a matter of fact, I just finished cleaning out my desk, and now I'm taking my pictures off the wall. I've been 'let go,' as they say."

"Oh," said David, trying to sound sympathetic, although he thought Rachel and her talents were wasted at the News. "I'm sorry."

"Don't be," replied Rachel. "I'm glad. Time for something new. See you soon."

David redeemed his car from the airport parking lot then headed south on Interstate 5. After thirty minutes of bumper-to-bumper madness, he exited and wound his way toward Rachel's house. En route he stopped at a gift shop where he bought a small bottle of expensive perfume.

As he pulled up to the neat clapboard house, Rachel came running out to meet him. He climbed out of the car and into her arms, their mouths meeting hungrily, bodies pressed together in an erotic embrace. Minutes passed before Rachel finally drew back.

"We'd better go inside," she giggled. "What will the neighbors think?"

Once inside, David grabbed Rachel and spun her around, pulling her close to him and kissing her once again with urgency. Rachel, caught by surprise, gasped and let out a soft, sweet murmur of pleasure. They sank slowly to the floor, holding each other tightly, forgetting about everything except their desire for each other.

Sometime later, they broke apart and stared deep into each other's eyes.

"I missed you," whispered David.

Rachel rubbed against him teasingly. "I can tell," she said. "Maybe it's time for a cooling-off period. Why don't we go get something to eat? Do you mind walking a few blocks?"

Although the temperature was mild, a soft drizzle was falling, so David and Rachel donned lightweight jackets. Rachel tied her hair back into a ponytail and put on a black baseball cap with "Pole Sitters" embroidered in red on the front.

"Pole Sitters?" questioned David when he saw it.

"It's a souvenir from a charity softball game I played in years ago when I worked at the local cable company. The people in management made up one team, the 'Pencil Pushers'; the installers — the 'Pole Sitters were the other team."

"You were an installer? You mean you actually climbed up the telephone poles?"

"Yeah, I was the only woman on the crew." Seeing the incredulous look in David's eyes, Rachel laughed. "I'm not exactly your typical woman, I guess.

"That's one of the things I love about you," said David admiringly.

David and Rachel walked down to the main boulevard where they turned south and continued several blocks before ducking into a corner Café. Rachel ordered for them both: tuna melts with ranch fries, huge dill pickles, and homemade baked beans.

As they waited for their meal, they filled each other in on the events of the last couple days.

"I'm dying to know what happened in Vegas?" asked Rachel.

"No, you first. What happened at work?"

"Oh, well, just what everyone predicted. The News is no more. The Seattle Times, which acquired it recently, has decided to go in 'another direction,' whatever that means. I love those euphemisms. But I don't care. In fact, I feel excited, like a door has opened, not closed."

She interrupted her monologue as the waiter, a goateed young man with a deformed left arm, served their meals with an ease born of experience. After refilling their water glasses and slapping the check down on the table, he commanded "Enjoy!' and moved on to another table.

Rachel reached for the ketchup and generously slathered the potatoes before popping a fry into her mouth. "Okay, now what about you?" she asked through a mouthful of potato.

David relayed the details of his Vegas trip, neither embellishing nor diminishing the narrow escape he and Dick had had.
Rachel was not fooled, however, immediately realizing what a dangerous spot they'd been in. "You could have been seriously hurt, even killed," she protested. "Do you enjoy putting yourself at risk like that?"

"To tell you the truth, it never mattered much before, admitted David. It was just a job that needed to be done, and I was good at it. I never considered that I might lose something, because there was nothing to lose." He reached across the table and laced his fingers through Rachel's. "Things are different now: I have you to think about." Rachel tightened her fingers around his. "Yes, you do. I'd be pretty mad at you if you got hurt, and believe me, you don't want me mad at you."

David looked at her, bemused. "Really? Just what do you do to people who tick you off?"

Rachel didn't hesitate. "I make them sorry that they did whatever they did — maybe not today, maybe not tomorrow, but as Humphrey Bogart once said, soon and for the rest of their lives."

"Sounds ominous. Would this be your one-character flaw?"

Rachel laughed. "Well, I'm sure it's not my only one, and obviously I'm being overly dramatic. But I do believe people should be considerate to one another. I think of life as this big game, and for the game to work we've all got to play fair. When I catch someone cheating, it really gets my blood boiling, I try to make sure they don't get away with it."

David looked at her in mock horror. "What do you do? Put out a contract on them?"

Rachel rolled her eyes. "Of course, not — that would be too expensive. And, besides, unscrupulous people usually hang themselves, given the right rope." She bit into her tuna melt, chewing thoughtfully. "Here's a good example: A couple of years ago, the job I have now — Director of Personnel came open, and a number of candidates applied. When the dust cleared, management had narrowed the field down to me and another woman at the paper. She ended up getting the job because she began an affair with the publisher, something I learned about from inside sources. I wouldn't have minded so much except this same woman made some rather unflattering remarks around the office about me, how I never would have been able to handle the job. So, when the company picnic rolled around, and I was chatting with the publisher's wife, I made an innocent remark about how great it was that the Director of Personnel got to go on business trips with the publisher. And that was the end of her."

David leaned back in his chair and laughed heartily.

"I see what you mean," he said appreciatively. "As long as we're sharing deep, dark secrets about ourselves, I should tell you that I seem to have a knack for getting myself into trouble."

Rachel looked at him with uncertainty. "Like, going-to jail kind of trouble?"

David smiled and shook his head. "No, I mean danger and disaster seem to follow me around. Ever since I was little, I've been getting myself into situations that have not only hurt me but should have killed me."

"Like what?" asked Rachel, slicing her dill pickle into bite-sized pieces. "Meeting criminals at deserted warehouses while carrying large amounts of cash?"

"No, that was nothing," shrugged David, licking the last of the tuna melt off his fingers. "It started when I was three and I fell down an abandoned well; it took the fire department several hours to get me out of that one. A few years later, I survived a small-plane crash. I've had a building fall on me, an avalanche buried me, and a car crash put me in the hospital for months."

Rachel looked at him in disbelief. "But you look so healthy, so strong, so. . . so. . .good!"

David chuckled, his eyes crinkling with pleasure at the compliment. "Well, I've done a lot of rehab work, but my real secret is my guardian angel."

"Your guardian angel?" repeated Rachel, unsure as to how serious he was. "I've always liked the idea that some benevolent spirit is watching out for me. But I don't know if I really believe it's true."

"Well, when you hear all I've been through, you will believe," said David. "I am convinced I would be dead by now if I hadn't had some kind of divine protector. But I don't expect to have that help for much longer."

Rachel looked at him quizzically. "Why do you say that? Does that mean you're going to start leading a safe and sane life?"

"I doubt it. But a while ago I made a deal with God that if I found my soulmate, I would give back my guardian angel for someone else in need." He gazed at Rachel steadily as he said this, and there was no mistaking exactly what he meant.

David paid the bill and he and Rachel stepped back out into the rain, now coming down more insistently than when they had entered the Café. They huddled together, walking arm in arm as they hurried back to Rachel's house. Once inside, they hung up their coats in the mud room, and Rachel started to build a fire.

"Let me do that for you," offered David.

"Thanks, but this is one chore I enjoy. Why don't you go into the kitchen and open the bottle of wine I have chilling in the fridge?"

Two minutes later, David returned to the living room with an expensive chardonnay and two long-stemmed wine glasses. The fire had roared to life with the torrid first flames that come from newspaper and kindling. Rachel and David settled comfortably on the couch. As Rachel poured the wine, David took a small box from under the cushion where he had hidden it earlier.

"To celebrate your opening a new door," he said as he presented it to Rachel.

Rachel looked up at him in surprise, her expressive dark eyes wide in wonder. She slowly undid the ribbon, lifted the lid to the box, and exclaimed with delight when she discovered the distinctive ice-blue perfume bottle inside.

"Oh, David, I love this stuff! How did you know?"

David gazed into her eyes. "You keep forgetting, I've known you for a long, long time."

Rachel lifted a hand to his face, letting her fingertips caress the curve of his cheek. Then she leaned toward him for a long, sensuous kiss. When she finally pulled back, she said solemnly, "I'm beginning to think you have."

They spent the rest of the evening sipping the chardonnay and sharing secrets as they gazed into the glowing embers of the fire. Finally, David rose to go.

"Tomorrow I want to take you somewhere. Are you free?"

Rachel laughed. "Gee, let me check my schedule," she joked. Then, wrapping her arms around David's waist, she said, "I think it's to say that I can fit you in." Her sloe-eyed look said that he could take what she said in more than one way.

"Good. I'll pick you up at ten. Dress casual and wear tennis shoes."

At ten the next morning, David drove into Rachel's driveway to find her waiting outside for him, waving at him and jumping up and down like an excited child.

He climbed out of the car quickly, gave her a kiss, and then ushered her into the passenger side of the car. After he slid in behind the wheel, he turned to her with an inquiring smile.

"What was that?" he asked.

"What?" she asked, no hint of understanding in her face.

"You were jumping up and down."

Rachel put her hands over her eyes and gave a little groan.

"Was I?" She looked at David, obviously embarrassed. "It's something I've done ever since I was a kid. I don't even realize I'm doing it most of the time."

"I like it," David said. "It's spontaneous and real — you just being yourself. Too many people put on an act, try to be like everyone else so others will think they're cool."

"Oh, so now I'm not cool," teased Rachel. "I'm some kind of dork, is that it?"

"You are you. You don't pretend to be anything you're not. That is one of the finest traits a person can have, in my opinion," replied David.

Twenty minutes later, the blue BMW exited the Alaskan Viaduct to cruise along Seattle's picturesque waterfront and then turn into the holding lot at the ferry terminal. There Rachel and David waited in the car to board the ferry for the short trip across the Sound to Bainbridge Island.

More and more, David and Rachel found themselves feeling free and easy in each other's presence. As they sat in the car awaiting the arrival of the ferry, their animated conversation ranged far and wide. At one point, Rachel talked about a book she had recently read and found fascinating because of its controversial subject.

"It challenges the accepted accounts of the beginnings of the Christianity as we know it. Some of what it claims is pretty shocking, talking about conspiracy and betrayal and murder great stuff," she explained. After a moment, she continued, the slightest bit of apprehension creeping into her voice. "That's one thing we haven't talked about yet."

"What?" asked David. "Religion?"

"Well, for some people it can make or break a relationship," she said, still not sure whether she wanted to pursue the subject.

David was quiet for a few minutes, thinking about it. "Yes, I suppose that's true. But I tend to think in terms of spirituality rather than religion."

Rachel's response was immediate and obviously relieved. "Me too! I haven't been to church for ages, but I'm always having conversations with God."

David took her hand, smiling at her. "And what does He say?" he asked with amusement.

Rachel drew her hand back quickly as though offended. "First of all, it isn't a "he." And, secondly..."

she started to giggle. "Secondly, she gives me all sorts of divine direction."

David looked at Rachel for a long moment and then leaned over to open the glove compartment. "I want to show you something," he said in a quiet voice, suddenly turning serious. His fingers searched the back of the glove compartment; among the sundry pens and pencils, ferry schedules and gas receipts, he found what he was looking for. He drew it out and turned his hand over, letting Rachel see what rested in his palm.

"Oh!" she gasped, and then she reached down to pick up the small silver crucifix that lay there. She turned it over in her hand, wonder spreading across her face. "This is exactly like the one on my key chain," she whispered. "Mine belonged to my grandfather who passed away twenty years ago. He was a great old guy, a real character. I carry it around because it reminds me of him."

David nodded. "I figured it was something like that because I haven't ever seen another one like it. Mine was my mother's, the only thing I have of hers. To me it's more a link to my past than a religious symbol."

David and Rachel stared into each other's eyes, both thinking that this was just another sign that they were destined for each other. Suddenly, the deep bellow from the horn of the arriving ferry broke their concentration and focused their attention on loading.

Following the hand signals of a uniformed ferryman, David squeezed the car into a space on the lower level of the ferry; then he and Rachel climbed the two flights of stairs to the observation deck where they took in one of the most spectacular views anywhere in the world. The rain of the night before had abated, but a few dark-gray thunderheads with billowing white crowns still moved sluggishly across the sky. The glass and steel of the downtown skyscrapers contrasted appealingly against the rugged backdrop of the Cascade Mountains. And majestic Mount Rainier, wearing its icy snowcap like a monarch's mantle, reigned imposingly over the bustling metropolis below.

When the ferry docked on the other side, David followed the line of cars off the ferry and onto the highway that dissected the island.

"Where to now?" asked Rachel.

"You'll see."

David soon turned off the main highway onto a less traveled street. From here he followed meandering and increasingly smaller roads until finally they were crawling along on a narrow, gravelly path just wide enough for the car. Tall conifers and dense brush kept out most of the sunlight, making it seem as though they had stumbled into the primeval forest of legendary fairytales. And then, suddenly, the trees gave way to a wide green meadow that offered a sunny pastoral scene, complete with grazing cows and split-rail fencing. At the edge of the meadow, overlooking the sound, perched a white-washed cottage with a thatched roof.

"Where are we?" gasped Rachel.

"The Conservatoire," answered David.

He parked the car and both he and Rachel climbed out. He came around the car and put his arm on her shoulder, nestling her against him. They stood like that for a few moments, appreciating the natural beauty surrounding them.

"This property belongs to the University of Washington," explained David. "It's used for a number of independent research projects. But it's open to the public, and the cottage actually offers some amenities for visitors. Come on, I'll show you."

They went inside where they spent a few minutes enjoying an exhibit on the different flora and fauna found on the island. After contributing a few dollars to the Conservatoire fund, David helped himself to tea and cookies for both of them, and they sat in a nook facing a massive picture window, watching for signs of life on the sound.

"This place is enchanting," said Rachel. "I feel like we're tucked away from the rest of the world, all alone in our secret hideaway."

"Well, don't get too comfortable, because we're going for a hike." At Rachel's look of alarm, he assured her, "Don't worry, it won't be very strenuous. You'll be fine."

They finished their snack and returned to the car where David strapped on the backpack he had stowed in the trunk. Rachel retrieved her hooded sweatshirt, which she tied around her waist, and donned a pair of Ray-ban sunglasses.

"Follow me," said David.

They walked along a footpath that paralleled the fence until they came to a trailhead that headed into the trees. For the next hour they tramped at a leisurely pace, following a track that wandered in and out of the forest. Along the way they stopped frequently to examine the many little-known wonders of this still-untouched preserve. Finally, their trail took a steep upward turn and then emptied out onto the crest of a bluff overlooking the water.

"Ready for a break?" asked David as he slid the pack off his back. Unzipping the main compartment, he took out a large blanket and spread it out on the ground. Next came picnic plates and a thermos, followed by an assortment of gourmet snacks.

Rachel kneeled down on the blanket and helped him arrange the goodies; when all was ready, they dug in hungrily. A half an hour passed before their eating slowed, their hunger finally satisfied.

"What a wonderful idea it was to come here," Rachel said contentedly as she sipped a cup of coffee. A ray of sun peeked from behind a cloud, warming her back through her thin T-shirt.

"I knew you'd like it," said David. "At least, I hoped you would. I love the quiet, the serenity, the beauty... it's one of my favorite places in the world." He busily packed up the food and cleared away the plates and other debris, neatly arranging everything back in the pack. Then, moving close to Rachel, he gently took her cup and set it on the ground and eased her down onto the blanket where he pinned her hands above her head. Rachel did not resist. Instead she closed her eyes and met his lips eagerly, losing herself in the delicious thrill of the moment.

David released one of her hands, and for the first time since they had met, he allowed himself the pleasure of exploring her body. He softly caressed her face, fingers flowing down her neck, pausing at her throat, and slowly continuing to the firm roundness of her breast. A little moan escaped Rachel's lips, but she did not move. David's hand lingered there briefly, and then continued downward, across her rib cage and abdomen until it reached her inner thigh, which he gently stroked. He pulled his lips from Rachel's, watching her fluttering eyelids, and smiled.

"Are you enjoying this as much as I am?" he asked her, his voice husky and breathless.

" . . . Hmm," Rachel murmured as though she were under a spell. Her eyelids opened, and she focused on him intently, a devilish gleam in her eye. "Why don't you lie down here next to me, and I'll show you what it feels like." David did as he was told. Touching her had awakened his desire for her and he could no longer fight the powerful sexual urge that consumed him. He lay down on his back, closed his eyes, and awaited the sweet fire that would come with Rachel's touch. What he felt, instead, was a big, fat raindrop spattering onto his forehead.

Rachel ignored the erratic raindrops and followed his lead, mirroring the way he had touched her. She kissed his ear and stroked his face, using her short, polished nails to add an enticing bite to her touch.

Plop! Another raindrop found David's face. Plop! Plop! Oh, God, thought David. Not now.

Rachel's fingers had found the chest hair that peeked out of his shirt collar. Just as she began to undo the next button, the sky opened up and the rain came down with a vengeance.

David opened his eyes and sat up. "Should I take this as a sign?" he asked Rachel, laughing in spite of himself. "Maybe we're not supposed to make love."

Rachel stood up, pulling David with her. "I think we're just being told not to do it here," she said. She helped David fold up the blanket. He jammed it into the pack, which he slid hastily onto his shoulders, and they trotted toward the shelter of the trees and the path that would lead them back to the car.

This time they sprinted down the path, making it back to the car in less than thirty minutes. Once inside, they looked at each other and laughed. They were soaked to the skin and splattered with mud. David pulled a pine needle out of Rachel's hair.

"You look very sexy," he said, his eyes taking in the wet T-shirt which now clung to her like a second skin.

He started the car and turned the heater on full-blast. Within a few minutes, they were back at the intersection with the main highway. Rachel expected David to turn right, which would take them back to the ferry. Instead, he turned left.

"And now where are you taking me?" she asked.

"We're going to get out of these wet clothes."

David continued to drive north along the highway until they crossed a bridge that brought them onto the Kitsap Peninsula. From there Rachel knew that they could eventually make a loop around the south end of the sound and return home without the ferry ride. But David had other plans. Upon entering the hamlet of Poulsbo, he turned off the highway and into the parking lot of a motel overlooking the water.

"Be right back," he said.

A few minutes later, he returned to the car and drove it to the parking spot in front of the very last room of the motel block. As he and Rachel entered Room 15, she uttered a cry of delight. Beyond the simple, attractive furnishings that greeted them lay a patio with a breathtaking view of the bay. A cozy couch faced a brick fireplace flanked by stacks of kindling and wood. And a spacious bathroom featured a jacuzzi and two-person sauna.

Rachel turned to David, put her arms around him, and kissed him. "Now it's my turn to say I'll be right back. "

She walked into the bathroom and closed the door. David heard the sound of the shower briefly as he stacked the kindling and wood. Just as he had the fire lit, Rachel emerged from the bathroom. Her hair was pulled back, accentuating her large eyes and high cheekbones. She wore nothing but a bath towel.

Without a word, she walked over to David, took his hand, and led him to the queen-sized bed. Slowly and lovingly, she removed his clothes, until he lay completely naked before her. She gently pushed him down on the bed and began to touch him. She started with his chest, lingering on the nipples, then moved down to his navel and then further on down to his thighs. She touched him everywhere but where he most wanted her to, bringing him to the edge of orgasm. When she stopped, he opened his eyes questioningly; she smiled at him and stood up, letting the towel fall to the floor.

David stared oneself-consciously, openly admiring Rachel's firm but nicely curved body. Her naturally olive skin was tanned in most places, which served to highlight her breasts and lower abdomen where the skin had remained untouched by the sun. With a deliberateness that only served to intensify their passion, Rachel lowered herself onto David and they began a slow rhythmic dance, bringing each other time and time again to the brink of climax, so that when they could resist no more, the explosion they felt was unlike any other they had ever known. Rachel cried out in pleasure, and David grunted and growled like the lion she envisioned him to be.

Afterward they lay entwined in each other's arms, saying nothing for a while, simply content to be close. Finally, David broke the silence.

"I love you," he whispered as he kissed her hair. "You are everything and more than the woman of my fantasies. I want to be with you always." He pulled back a bit so that he could look down into her warm brown eyes. "Will you marry me?"

Before Rachel answered, David could hear her answer joyously ringing inside his head.

"Yes," she said simply. And with a renewed passion and intensity, they began their lovemaking once again.

CHAPTER 11

The next few days passed quickly for David and Rachel as they made plans to merge their lives. Both agreed that they wanted to marry as soon as possible, and they decided on the evening of the following Friday to exchange their solemn vows.

Rachel suggested an intimate wedding, with just the closest of family and friends attending. This suited David, since he had few friends and almost no family. The people he cared for most, his foster parents, were traveling around the country in their motor home; he had no idea where they were or how to get ahold of them. And he had completely lost touch with his only sibling, an older sister who had gone to New York several years ago to be in the theatre. He did want to invite Dick Sloane and Terry Patrick, the latter whom he planned to ask to be his best man. David had last seen Terry when he had driven his friend home from the hospital in Ellensburg. Since then, he had spoken to Terry a couple of times and the powerlifter had assured him that he was recovering nicely from the heart attack. But David had been unable to reach him for the past three weeks and suspected that Terry was spending a lot of time in Ellensburg.

Once they had decided on the date, Rachel threw herself into making the wedding arrangements. The first thing she did was to call her parents with the news.

Her father didn't like the idea too well at first. "Good God, Rachel, you haven't known him very long," he protested. "It took you years to decide to marry Michael, and even then, you couldn't go through with it. How can you be so sure about this guy if you've only known him a few weeks?"

"That's just the point, Dad," Rachel countered. "Michael was never right for me, and I spent years trying to convince myself otherwise. With David, I knew almost immediately that he was the man I've been waiting for."

Her dad wasn't' giving up that easily. "But, Rachel, don't you think you should wait and "Oh, hush, Walter," interrupted his wife of forty years who was listening on the extension in their bedroom. "You've probably forgotten that you hadn't known me more than a month when you proposed marriage. I admit it took us a bit longer to get to the altar, but we were younger. David and Rachel are mature adults; they know what they're doing."

A resigned sigh floated across the line. "All right, baby, if that's what you want. You make the arrangements and send me the bill," her dad said, and then added with mock sternness, "and no backing out this time!"

Next Rachel called a small retreat center, The Pines, which was nestled in a mountain glen close enough to the famed Snoqualmie Falls to feel its spray. With a little negotiating, she managed to get permission to have the wedding on their lawn, where the falls would provide a dramatic backdrop. The Pines also had a cozy, wood paneled library that could be used for the celebratory dinner afterward, which Rachel arranged to be catered by a swank Seattle eatery.

One night, as they shared a quick dinner at a café, Rachel brought David up to date on the plans. She chattered on with excited animation, oblivious to David's bemused expression as he listened patiently. When she finally paused to take a bite of her clam chowder, David shook his head, as though it were all too much for him.

"Just tell me when and where, and I'll be there," he told her with a wink.

"You'd better," retorted Rachel. "Oh, listen, one thing I would like you to do is get fitted for your suit. What would you think about tails?"

"Tails!" cried David. "I thought we were going for the informal look."

"All right, maybe not a tail, but I think it would be nice to wear something special. There's this neat little shop down on Second that has all sorts of men's wear for special occasions. The man who owns it said if we came in on Wednesday, he could have something ready by Friday."

"Well, I can't let you pick it out all by yourself."

"Why not? Do I get to help you pick out your wedding dress?"

Rachel blushed. "I've already got it."

"Already?" asked David in surprise. "With your taste I can't believe you bought something right off the rack.' Then he paused, sudden comprehension flickering in his eyes. "Of course, you already have a dress — the one from your wedding with Michael, right?"

Rachel shook her head. "No, I got rid of that dress the very next day. This is a different one — one I made myself."

"But we only decided to do this five days ago. When did you have time?"

Rachel's complexion grew redder. "If you must know, I designed and constructed it for a bridal fashion show I helped produce last year. I just never knew whether I'd have a chance to wear it."

"Then I guess I'm doing you a big favor," David kidded her, to which she gave him a kick under the table.

Later that evening as they relaxed back at Rachel's house, she brought out a worn, leather-bound book with a broken lock.

"My diary," she explained. "I wrote in it mostly during my teens."

She opened the diary and thumbed through the pages, stopping when she found what she was looking for.

"Here, read this." She handed the diary to David and pointed to an entry dated July 13, 1978. There David found the wistful ramblings of a teenage girl writing about the man of her dreams. Even at that young age, Rachel had had a clear vision of the person she hoped would come into her life. She described him as kind and gentle, but possessing great strength — in both body and mind.

She pictured him as having long, wavy hair, rugged features, and a muscled physique, an image that prompted her to call him her Lion.

As he pored over the words, David felt as though he were reading about himself, the physical and philosophical traits of this dream man, written nearly twenty years ago, describing him uncannily.

"I can't believe it," David said, putting the diary down and looking up at Rachel who had been reading over his shoulder. "It's almost like you were writing about me.

Rachel moved around the couch and eased herself onto his lap. Putting her arms around him, she whispered against his lips, "I was, my darling Lion, I was."

Although David had few responsibilities for the wedding, he was busy with other duties. He and Rachel had decided that it made sense for him to move into her house, which meant he had to go through all the tedious chores that come with moving. He arranged to have most of his furniture and other belongings put in storage until he and Rachel found a larger place to live. His computer and other office paraphernalia were moved into Rachel's spare bedroom; though it was a tight squeeze. Next, he gave notice on his condo and arranged for the utilities and the phone to be shut off at the end of the week. And, finally, he made the honeymoon arrangements, a two-week island-hopping cruise in the Caribbean.

He couldn't wait for Rachel and him to begin their life together, and he marveled at how they had found each other at just the right time. Both were at a crossroads in their professional lives: Rachel was unemployed, and David was tired of muscle-man jobs and haggling with strangers over the phone. The two of them spent much of their time together talking about the future, what direction their professional lives might take, and whether they could pursue a career path together. Their future seemed bright with unlimited possibilities.

The Tuesday night before the wedding, David was back in his condo, now stripped of nearly everything. He still had his phone and a few things in the fridge, but that was it. He had come back this evening to do some last-minute cleaning and make a few repairs and would spend the night atop an air mattress burrowed in his down-filled North Face sleeping bag. Tomorrow he would move into Rachel's house for good.

David was fast asleep when, a little after I A.M., the shrill peal of the phone jolted him awake. He reached for the receiver in the dark, first dropping it then fumbling for it noisily as it skidded around on the floor. Finally, he found it and lifted it to his ear.

"Rachel?" he mumbled sleepily into the phone.

"Geez, who is this woman?" came the familiar gruff voice over the line. "This is the second time you've mistaken me for her."

David gave his head a shake, trying to clear away the fuzziness. "Jack?"

"Yep. Hey, sorry it took so long for me to get back to you. But if you saw where I lived you would understand why I have such a hard time communicating."

David sat up, leaning back against the wall in the living room where he had been sleeping. He reached for the bedside flashlight and turned it on.

"Just where are you, Jack?"

"Down in Colombia, sitting almost smack-dab on top of the equator."

"Colombia? I thought you were supposed to be in Africa, chasing birds you were going to export."

"I did, but the competition there was stiff. I couldn't get anywhere because the market was all tied up and nobody wanted to cut me in. Then I met this guy from Colombia, and he told me that there were more birds in his country alone than in all of Africa, but there weren't many exporters. So, I came on over, and you know what? He was right. I tell you I got a good thing going here."

"You're always telling me you're onto a good thing," said David. Jack was the eternal optimist, forever thinking he was on the road to making a fortune. But he was a good businessman, too, so David was inclined to believe most of what he said. "What about Diane?" David asked, referring to Jack's longtime love. "Does she like it down there?"

"Well, she did when she was here, but she had to go back up to the States. That's one of the reasons I'm calling you. You see, what I've got right now is a very rough operation for bird exportation. But I've made plans to improve it, and that takes money. So, Diane is back up in Seattle, working at the veterinary hospital and sending me the capital to make this thing go. I'm telling ya, David, there's big bucks in this business."

David said nothing, waiting for what he knew was coming. Jack was his dearest friend in the world, and he understood only too well just how his mind worked. David would have laid odds that Jack was going to try to get him to come down to Colombia.

"What I really need is a partner, someone who isn't afraid to put in some hard work for a big financial payback. Someone with business savvy. Someone I can trust." Jack paused. "Someone like you."

"Oh, I don't think you mean someone like me," replied David, good-natured sarcasm creeping into his voice. "You mean me.

"Well, you'd be great at this. I'll tell ya, it's wild down here. Bird hunting is a kick; you'd love it. And I have this huge plantation in

the middle of the rain forest where I live with Captain Nemo, and
—" "Who?"

"Oh, you'll find out when you get here. But, here's the deal. I
need someone pretty quick. I'd cut you in as an equal partner if you
could come down and work without pay for six months. By then I
should be able to have everything built so that I can not only house
and export birds, but act as my own quarantine station as well.
What do you think?" David shook his head. Same old Jack.

"Well, I don't know what to think. A few weeks ago, I would have
been on the next flight, but things have changed."

"David," said Jack, suspicion in his voice, "please don't tell me
you're gonna pass up this opportunity because of a woman.

"No," said David, "I'm gonna pass it up because of a wife."

"No, shit! You're married?"

"Not yet, but I will be in less than three days."

Hoots of laughter came across the line. "I gotta meet this chick,"
said Jack. "God, the woman who caught you must be somethin'
else."

"Believe me, she is," said David.

"All right, well listen, let me leave this phone number with you.
It rings through to the local post office and they'll take a message
for me. Talk it over with — what's her name again?"

"Rachel."

"Talk it over with Rachel. This could be a good thing for both of
you."

David took the number and, after promising to get back to Jack
before he left on his honeymoon, he hung up.

As he drifted off to sleep, David thought about bird hunting in
the Colombian jungle, and he had to admit it did sound exotic, even

appealing. He had always thought of himself as a bit of an adventure seeker, and he loved to take on a new challenge.

Who knows? he thought to himself. Maybe Rachel will like the idea. And with that, he let his thoughts of The Black lull him into dreamland.

The next morning, David arose early and called Rachel first thing to talk about what she had scheduled for the day. "Hey, I missed you last night," she said softly into the phone.

"I missed you too. But then I dreamt about you all night long," said David.

"Were they sweet dreams?"

"Sweaty dreams is more like it," laughed David. "You've got a lot to live up to next time I get you in bed."

Rachel giggled and then turned her attention to their plans for the day. "I'm going to the florist in a few minutes, and we have that appointment at the clothiers at eleven. Do you want to meet there?"

"I was hoping to catch a quick workout at the gym, so that would be great." David wrote down the address and directions to the clothing shop and promised Rachel he'd be there on time.

A half an hour later, David stood in his doorway and surveyed the apartment for the last time. Then, after dropping his keys in the landlord's mail slot, he climbed into the Beemer and drove the few miles to the Westside Gym. Although he went through each phase of his workout faithfully, David's mind was elsewhere, filled with heady thoughts of the exciting changes that were about to take place in his life. At one point he went over to his gym bag for a drink from his water bottle, and so intent was he in his own thoughts that when someone touched his arm, he jumped a foot in the air.

"Wow!" said a friendly voice. "If I were an Olympics judge I've given you a nine on that jump."

David turned around to see Terry standing there, a big grin on his face.

"Hey, I've been trying to get ahold of you," said David.

"I know, I know. I haven't been around too much lately. Been spending a lot of time over in Ellensburg."

David nodded his head, a knowing look on his face. "Jill" was all he said.

"Yeah, Jill. I'll tell you what, she is the best thing that ever happened to me. I am head over heels for her. You saw how I didn't want to leave her when I was released from the hospital."

David smiled, remembering the long kisses and tearful goodbyes the two had shared in the hospital parking lot.

"I have never clicked like this with anyone before," Terry continued. "I'm probably going to move over there permanently. I want to be with her all the time. It's crazy — so crazy I'm even thinking about marriage, if you can believe that!"

David laughed. "I believe it, 'cause the same thing's happened to me. I'm getting married."

"What! Well, congratulations!" Terry grabbed David in a big bear hug, squeezing all of the air out of David's lungs. When Terry finally released him, it took David a few moments to get his breath back.

"That's why I've been calling you," David said when he could finally speak. "It's kind of a spur-of-the-moment wedding, very informal. I was hoping you could come, maybe even stand up for me as my best man."

Terry slapped David on the back. "Nothin' I'd like more. When is it?"

David pulled a pen and a small spiral-bound notebook out of his gym bag and wrote down the particulars for Terry. Then, with another bear hug and a promise to be there, Terry left David to finish his workout.

Forty-five minutes later, David was sitting behind the wheel of his car, driving to the clothier's. Since he was a few minutes early, he decided to swing by Rachel's, just in case she was there, hoping they could go together.

When David pulled up to her house, he didn't see the Jaguar, but he knocked on the door to be sure she wasn't home. When Rachel didn't appear, he climbed back in the car and headed down to Second Avenue.

Once again, his mind wandered, and as he traveled along the main thoroughfare, he didn't pay much attention when the traffic slowed to a halt just prior to the bridge that spanned a local tributary of the Green River.

Suddenly, something jolted David out of his preoccupation. He looked around him, acutely aware that something was terribly wrong.

He looked at his watch: 10:55 A.M. blinked at him in effervescent green numerals. He sat for another minute, a terrible feeling of fear engulfing him. What is it? he wondered. Being stopped here in traffic, a seemingly common occurrence, was filling him with a dreadful feeling of foreboding.

And then the cars ahead of him started to move, slowly crossing the bridge one at a time. When his turn came, David saw the cause for the delay. A sheriff's car had blocked off the far-right lane, and an officer was directing two lanes to merge into one. As he drove by, David saw that the last few feet of the guardrail on the bridge were mangled and bent, as though a car had plowed through it.

Terror gripped David's heart. At his first opportunity, he pulled the BMW over to the side of the road and ran back to the chewed place in the guardrail. He leaned over and looked down to the water's edge. There he saw what he had feared most: the overturned carcass of a vintage green Jaguar.

"Oh, God!" screamed David. "Where is she, where?"
He moved around the guardrail and started down the embankment, where he was intercepted by one of the officers at the scene.

"Go home," the officer said. "You don't want to see this."
"Where is she?" David screamed again, and with a quick move he broke the officer's hold and flipped him onto the ground. He continued down the slope until he was stopped in his tracks by the sight of a figure hanging in the branches of a scrub oak tree. It was Rachel, blood dripping down her face and into a dark pool a few feet below her on the ground.

David couldn't believe his eyes. "Rachel!" he screamed, and he started to run toward her but was quickly held back by two more officers. As he watched helplessly, a paramedic shrouded her entire body in a khaki-green blanket. "I'm sorry," he said. "She's dead."

"Aahhhhhh!!!!" David's scream filled the air and he violently shook off the two officers who frantically tried to contain him. Instead of charging down the bank to Rachel's body, however, he ran back upward, blindly heading to his car, tears streaming down his face. Once behind the wheel, he sobbed uncontrollably for several minutes.

Oh, God, he thought, how can you do this to me? He sat there for over an hour, crying, cursing, praying, finally quiet in the resignation that none of what he had wanted would ever be his.

Four hours later, David sat in a seat on a TWA jet bound for Colombia. Nothing was left for him here; he was on his way to a new life, an exciting life, a life that would help him forget about what he had lost. As though he ever could.

CHAPTER 12

Before David hopped a jet for Colombia, he had called the number Jack had given him, leaving the brief message that he was on his way down and would call again when he reached Bogota. Several hours later, after a brief layover and change of planes in Miami, David arrived in the capital city of Colombia.

David had spent those long hours traveling in wretched misery, oblivious to everything but his pain. He had spoken to no one on the flights, withdrawing completely into himself, his eyes closed, his heart and soul grieving. When he at last disembarked from the plane, he resolved to hide away his heartache and throw himself into this strange, new life.

The airport at Bogota was a zoo — crowded, chaotic, filled with unusual sights and smells. David found a pay phone and, after a few difficulties, was able to connect with Jack's message number.

"Ah, sī," said a man's friendly voice when David identified himself. "Senior Campbell left a message for you. You must go to the domestic terminal and look for a small
outfit called El Jején."

David thanked the man and hung up, then turned to look for a sign that might give him an idea as to which way to go. Because he knew very little Spanish, David sought out signs with international symbols rather than words. After thirty minutes of walking, riding trams, and negotiating escalators and stairs, he finally found his destination at the farthest end of the terminal.

He approached the check-in counter where two men, both wearing mismatched street clothes, were engaged in a heated discussion. David waited patiently until one of them noticed him.

"Sí?" asked the shorter, stockier of the two.

"I'm David Brooks. I think Jack Campbell arranged a flight for me?"

"Oh, Senior Brooks," the man said, smiling and grabbing David's hand in an enthusiastic handshake. "Welcome. I am Hector Aguirra. I was just speaking to our pilot, Pablo, on that very subject."

Pablo looked at David, the beginning of a scowl on his face.

"Is there a problem?" David asked, looking from one man to the other.

"No, no, we were discussing what else we could load onto the plane since there are no other passengers. But, since you are here and ready to go, Pablo can take you now."

Pablo picked up a duffle bag and jerked his head toward David, an invitation for him to follow. Instead of heading toward the boarding gates, however, Pablo walked to an exit door which led to an outside staircase and down to the tarmac.

David followed Pablo to a small, weathered, prop-engine airplane where Pablo indicated he should climb into the front passenger's seat. After tossing the duffle bag into the back of the cockpit, Pablo made himself comfortable in the pilot's seat and readied the plane for takeoff.

It suddenly occurred to David that he was in a strange country, about to take off in a rickety old plane flown by a mutinous pilot, headed to an unknown destination. Ordinarily, such a situation would have put him instantly on alert. But he felt nothing. He didn't much care if he lived or died. He was dead inside already.

For the next forty-five minutes, as the ancient prop bumped and sputtered on its course, he stared out the window at the changing terrain below him until he could see nothing but a carpet of tangled vegetation. Suddenly, a large clearing appeared, a dark-brown patch contrasting against the vibrant green of the jungle. Pablo started his descent; the field, evidently, was the local runway.

Despite the limitations of the little plane, Pablo made a smooth landing and taxied to the end of the field where a burly man stood waiting beside a beat-up beige Range Rover. As soon as the plane came to a stop, he hurried over and pulled open David's door.

"David! You made it!" Jack extended a hand to David to help him down as he jumped from the plane onto the muddy runway, then gave his friend quick hug.

"Yeah, that was quite a ride," said David, turning to Pablo to give him a little salute of thanks. Pablo nodded and actually smiled.

As they walked to the car, Jack put an arm around David's shoulders. Although he had no idea what had actually happened, Jack knew that something must have gone terribly wrong for David to show up so suddenly — and alone. One look at David's face had confirmed his fears, and he wanted to let his friend know he was ready and willing to listen and do whatever he could.

Once inside the Range Rover, Jack started the engine and set off down a fairly smooth dirt road.

"How far do we have to go?" asked David.

"Well, that depends. In actual mileage, not far. Timewise, about an hour."

"At least the road isn't too bad," commented David.

Jack burst into laughter. "Just wait!"

Minutes later, Jack made a right turn onto what could only be called an overgrown path, and for the next fifty minutes, the jeep bounced along, dipping into potholes the size of a hot tub, climbing over fallen trees, breaking through snarling vines. Finally, Jack turned onto a better maintained road.

"This is my driveway," he said proudly.

The "driveway" proved to be a half a mile long, ending at a large clearing where a roughly built structure stood. 'Hi, honey, we're home!' Jack bellowed with good humor. Then turning to David, he said, "Well, what do you think?" When David didn't answer right away, Jack hurriedly explained, "In case you can't tell, what you're lookin' at is a warehouse for birds. That little addition on the upper level is where I live."

David stared at the building and all he could think of was that it looked like an overgrown treehouse.

"Uh, it's. . . well, it looks like fun," he said, trying to sound enthusiastic.

Jack laughed. "I know, I'm not the carpenter you are. I just tried to improve on the structure that was here when I bought the place, but I can tell by your reaction that I did a pretty poor job."

"No," stammered David who didn't want to hurt Jack's feelings, "I'm sure you did a lot. Especially out here, in the middle of nowhere, it must be difficult to get supplies and help and... " David's voice trailed off.

Jack opened the door and climbed out of the car. "Well, here's the good news. Your first assignment is to remodel this place."
David's lips slowly curved into his first smile since Rachel's death. "Now that's something I can sink my teeth into."

Dinner that night consisted of fish, rice, and some unidentifiable vegetables, cooked on a camp stove by candlelight. Although Jack had a diesel generator, its use was generally confined to providing heat for the captive

birds and their babies. For light, Jack had pillar candles sprinkled throughout the living quarters.
Dining with them in his high chair was Captain Nemo, Jack's pet monkey. The Captain was much like an unpredictable child cute and funny one minute, mischievous and unruly the next. Tonight, he ate quietly for several minutes, then let Jack know he was finished by throwing a handful of carrots at him. David, who loved animals, found Captain Nemo to be a delightful surprise.

After dinner, the two men sat sipping steaming cups of coffee, some of the finest in the world.
"One of the few fringe benefits of living here," said Jack, hoisting his cup. "The best damn coffee for just pennies.

David thought about the last time he'd enjoyed a good cup of coffee. It had been at the neighborhood Café with Rachel. His eyes filled with tears.

"She's dead," he said without preamble.

"What?" came Jack's startled response.

"Rachel. She's dead." David relayed the sad story in brief detail. When he finished, he looked into Jack's stricken face. "I sat on the side of the road, wishing I were dead too, thinking all I wanted to do was disappear. And then I thought of you and your offer. Coming down here, being with you, it was the best thing that could have happened to me."

"David, jeez, I am so sorry," said Jack sympathetically. "If there's anything I can do, let me know." He shook his head in disbelief and a faraway look came into his eyes. "I don't know if I ever told you — I don't talk about it much — but I was married when I was young, just out of high school. We used to do all sorts of crazy stuff together you know, we were young and thought we were hot shit. Anyway, one weekend we went rafting down the Skagit River during the spring runoff. The river was really high — we should have never been on it.

The waves were more than we could handle, and our boat flipped. I made it to the bank, but my wife got pulled under. We found her a couple days later a way down the river. Man, I was devastated." He grew silent for a few moments, the unpleasant memory clouding his usually happy-go-lucky countenance. "So, if you want to talk, go ahead, get it all out. I'll be glad to listen. If you don't want to say anything, that's all right too. You need to grieve in your own way if you want to get whole again."

David nodded, unable to speak. While he was still overcome by sorrow, he was beginning to feel an odd sense of peace, as though living out in the wilds of the Colombian jungle was the perfect balm for his injured soul.

A little later, the two men turned in. David, who hadn't had any real rest for nearly thirty-six hours, didn't even notice the thin, hard mattress and omnipresent bugs, but immediately slipped into a deep, dreamless sleep.

A few hours later, in the dead of night, David awoke slowly to the sound of distant thunder. At first, he couldn't remember where he was. Then it all came back in a rush. He was somewhere in the middle of the Colombian jungle. Hovering at the edge of his consciousness was an undefined pain, a terrible weight depressing his soul. As his head cleared, so did his memory, and he suffered the shocking realization of what had happened all over again: Rachel was dead.

He closed his eyes as salty tears streamed down his cheeks. Is this what it's going to be like? he wondered. Reliving the horror of the accident over and over again? That seemed more than he could bear.

A flash of lightning lit the small room, followed closely by a loud thunderclap. Hard-driving rain began to pelt the tin roof, as though clamoring to be let inside. Indeed, the rain was coming in through the window which David had left open; quickly he climbed out his bed and walked across the room to lower and secure the sash. Then he stood there, gazing out at the storm, but seeing nothing, his thoughts on the woman he had loved and lost.

As swiftly as it had come, the storm moved on. Within a few minutes, a break in the clouds revealed a nearly full moon, its bright rays illuminating the landscape.

Suddenly David stood up straight, his attention focused on the patch of sky showing through the clouds.   It reminded him of something Rachel had once said. They had been walking home from their last dinner down at the Café when they had been treated to a beautiful violet sunset painting a sky filled with scattered puffy clouds. Through the clouds they could see ever-deepening hues of blue sky, creating the eerie effect that they were gazing into another dimension.

"Look, David," Rachel had said, "there's the way to heaven."
David now stared at the luminescent clouds and dark, star-filled sky. Perhaps Rachel was trying to tell him that she was in heaven. Although this thought didn't lessen his longing for her, still it comforted him. Finally, he moved back to his bed where exhaustion once again overcame him, and he fell back to sleep.

When David awoke the next morning, the sun was already rising in the sky. He felt a heaviness on his chest and opened his eyes to find Captain Nemo sitting there, his sharp-nailed fingers sticking up David's nose.

"Yuck!" screamed David, as he tossed Captain Nemo onto the floor. "What the hell are you doing!"
"You up, David?" Jack's voice floated up the stairs Nemo with you?"
"Yeah, and you wouldn't believe what he was doing!" David yelled down, still repulsed by the monkey's behavior.

Jack gave a throaty laugh that ended in a short fit of coughing. "I know what he was doing. Sorry. I lock him up at night, but he sometimes manages to get out."

Ten minutes later, David came down to a huge breakfast of eggs, some kind of cured meat, and assorted tropical fruits. He ate heartily, surprised by his appetite. Although the intense grief of losing Rachel hovered constantly in the background, David was finding that being a stranger in a strange land helped him push back the pain, almost as if meeting and losing Rachel had happened long ago in another lifetime.

After breakfast, Jack and David got down to business.

"Here's what I'd like you to do," explained Jack. "I want to expand and improve this operation, creating a facility that can house up to 2,000 birds and eggs. I see it as having four sections: one section — probably the largest in size where we keep cages with mature birds; an incubation area for the eggs; a nursery for the babies; and then a large quarantine station for exportation."

Jack reached into a side cupboard and drew out a large roll of papers. "Here's some rough plans I had drawn up," he said, unfurling the papers. For the next hour, he and David perused the blueprints, talking about the possibilities. Then Jack looked David straight in the eye. "I've got the money for the supplies, but I need you to make it happen," he said. "What do you think? Is that too much to put on you?"

David shook his head. "Right now, I think that's the best thing I could do," he replied. "You know how I love to build things. I can become so immersed in the project, I forget about everything else. And right now, there's nothing I'd rather do than forget."

"There's something else you need to know," confessed Jack, letting the papers spring back into a tight roll. "I've been having some health problems. I don't exactly know what's wrong — maybe nothing. Could be that I'm just too damn fat." He grabbed a chunk of the flabby flesh that peaked out from under his cotton shirt. "I've never weighed this much. Hell, I used to be in pretty good shape. Remember?"

David nodded. Although Jack had never been as avid about training as David was, he had worked out regularly when he'd lived in Seattle and had kept fairly fit.

"Lately, I don't seem to have any energy. I'm not sleeping well, and I've got some other minor symptoms that are not fit to discuss at the breakfast table. Anyway, next week I'm going into Bogota and some doctor there is gonna put me through a battery of tests. So, you'll be on your own.

"What about supplies?" asked David.

"I've already started working on that. Today we'll go over the list of necessary building materials. Tomorrow I'll introduce you to Tomás, the local trader who gets me everything I want or need — sooner or later," Jack added with a laugh.

Over the next several days, David threw himself into planning the remodeling of Jack's warehouse. He soon discovered that a sizable tributary of the Meta River ran along the eastern boundary of Jack's plantation, which was better than any highway for carrying freight. Here Tomás could easily make his deliveries by barge, unloading them on an ancient but sturdy dock. From there, a pair of oxen hauled the equipment, lumber, and just about everything else to the clearing near the warehouse.

The day came when David drove Jack to the airstrip, where Pablo sat waiting in the little prop plane.

"Take care, buddy," said Jack, giving David a big hug. "And don't try to build the Taj Majal in a day, okay?"

"Don't worry, I'll take it easy," lied David. He couldn't wait to get back to the plantation and start creating a warehouse and home that would make Jack proud.

Jack had figured he would be gone about a week. But one week stretched to two, then three, then four. He kept David updated on what was happening: tests and more tests were given, new doctors and specialists were brought in, then he was moved to another hospital with more sophisticated equipment. Time dragged on.

For David, the solitude was a gift, bringing him a much-needed time of renewal. Being on his own with a challenging project to occupy his mind was the perfect therapy. Although Rachel was never far from his thoughts, he tried mightily to keep the scene of the accident out his head, instead focusing on the vivid memories of their time together. He missed her terribly, but by calling to mind her beautiful image, her infectious giggle, her fiery spirit, he found a way to keep her with him. And, little by little, he started to heal.

David began to look forward to each new day with the intensity of a man possessed. He would arise at dawn and plan his goals for the day, and then dare himself to not just cross off each item on his list, but complete at least one additional task. Most days he succeeded; some days he was slowed down by the delayed arrival of supplies or an unexpected complication. And then there was Captain Nemo.

For the most part, the Captain behaved himself, following David around companionably and not being too much of a pest. But sometimes, such as when he managed to tear his diaper off and cavort around the house, disaster resulted.

One such incident scared David to death. He awoke around six, enjoying the fact that the monkey wasn't sitting on his chest as so often was the case. As David climbed out of bed, however, he noticed a trail of blood that led to one of the downstairs closets. Inside David found Captain Nemo huddled in pain, blood pouring from his mouth. On the floor sat David's double-edge razor, which the Captain had evidently mistaken for a toothbrush. Although the monkey's lips, gums, and tongue were covered with painful cuts, none were deep, and David cleaned him up and consoled him by breaking out a brand-new box of band aids the monkey's most cherished treasures.

Finally, after thirty-two days of hospital hell, Jack came home. When David picked up Jack at the airfield, he could see that his friend was tired, even haggard, from the ordeal.

"Hey, it's good to be home," said Jack, shaking David's hand. "How'd things go?"

"Well, okay, I guess," said David in a subdued voice as he threw Jack's duffle bag in the back seat of the Rover. "I didn't get as much done as I'd hoped I would, though."

"Ah, don't worry about it," said Jack, slowly climbing into the passenger's seat. "I'm back to help you now. We'll churn it out in no time."

David suppressed a smile. He had purposely downplayed what he had done to make his surprise all the more dramatic. As they drove into the clearing next to the warehouse, Jack let out a shriek.

"Jesus!" he cried. "Holy Mother of God! I can't believe it!"

The building that stood there bore no resemblance to the ramshackle treehouse he had left behind four weeks earlier. In its place stood what looked like a completely new building. The outside was sided in a grey vinyl, with attractive white trim around the windows. The inside had been reconfigured, sheet rocked, and painted. Heating ducts ran throughout, as did new wiring and plumbing. The warehouse downstairs had been cleaned out and organized into the sections Jack had wanted. Simple but effective systems for dispensing food and water to the birds were in place. Upstairs, two bathrooms had been added and the kitchen updated. Everything was either brand new or repainted and sparkling clean.

"You, you..." Jack sputtered, his face turning red. "Damn but you are the biggest bullshitter!" he finally managed to blurt out. He turned and gave David a bone crushing hug. "And the best friend a guy could ever have.' Jack turned back toward the building, and David thought he could see some vitality returning to his friend.

"Damn!" cried Jack again, heading inside. "Come on. Let's get to work!"

CHAPTER 13

That first evening home, Jack was like a kid with a new toy. David cooked dinner and listened with amusement as Jack began making plans, jumping excitedly from one idea to another, asking David his opinion only to dart to a new topic without waiting for an answer. It wasn't until they sat drinking their after-dinner coffee that David could see the adrenaline finally ebb from his friend's body as Jack sank wearily back into his chair.

"Bedtime," suggested David.

"Yeah, I'm bushed. Traveling home was brutal, not to mention the last four weeks of being poked and prodded like a guinea pig. I need to go to bed." Jack put his cup to his lips, inhaling the steamy aroma of the coffee. "It's just that I'm so damn excited about what you've done. I can really see how the business is going to work and I don't want to waste any more time.

"What's the next move?"

"We go get some birds!"

"We?" repeated David, his voice filled with skepticism.

"Are you going to be climbing up the trees?"

"Well, no, I thought that'd be your job, you are being so fit and all. But I'll be doing somethin' just as important." Seeing David's raised eyebrows, Jack explained, "I'll be on the ground with the binoculars, directing you toward the nests — and watching out for the angry mama birds so you'll have time to save your butt." "Oh, that's reassuring.

"Don't worry. I've done this before. It's a piece of cake. "

They decided that they'd spend the next day on a reconnaissance trip into the jungle to chart where the best hunting might be, then return early the following morning to try their luck.

The next morning, they set an easy pace, sleeping in late and enjoying a leisurely breakfast. It wasn't until noon that they climbed into the Range Rover and set out on their expedition.

"Let's go east first," suggested Jack. "I know a few spots I'd like to investigate."

"What exactly are we looking for?" asked David.

"Well, we're huntin' macaws — you know, like the one you bought from me. They nest in holes, usually in trees, but it could be in rocks on the side of a cliff or even in termite mounds. The most common varieties have either blue or gold plumage. But you want to be on the lookout for the white ones cause with those we more than double our profit."

The next four hours were spent traveling down bad roads that only got worse — pitted with potholes, covered with rocks, and overgrown with killer vines. Many a time they took off on foot, hacking their way through the thick vegetation, always looking skyward for the telltale signs of bird activity. It was hot, dirty work, but by late afternoon they'd found several promising sites to revisit the next day.

That evening at dinner, prompted by the effects of a bottle of good wine, Jack talked about what happened during his stay in Bogota.

"What they found wasn't good," he said, twirling a long-stemmed goblet in his fingers, one of the few fine things he had at in the house. "I've got prostate cancer. They put me through a program of drugs and radiation, but they're not too optimistic. I've got some medicine to take, but the fact is, I may be dying. I'm supposed to go back in a few weeks for a follow-up, so I guess I'll know more then." Jack lifted his glass and drained it. "Anyway, I'm not going to worry about it. Right now, I've got a business to build!"

David sat in stunned silence. He lowered his eyes to his glass of wine, so Jack wouldn't see the tears that had suddenly appeared. Jack had always been one of the most vital people David had known, living life large, never afraid of anything. He was the one who went off to Africa to catch wild animals, who rode his Harley with wild abandon, who had cheated death more than once.

"Come on, Jack, it's not gonna end like that for you, said David in what he hoped was an even, matter-of-fact voice. "You're destined to die some exotic death, crushed by a boa or falling out of an airplane."

Jack laughed. "Yeah, you're right, that's more my style.

Forget this cancer thing."

David raised his glass to make a toast. "To your continued good health — and a death that does you proud!"

The morning of the hunt found Captain Nemo on David's chest, rudely awakening him at 3:30 A.M. The rich smell of freshly brewed coffee drifted into his room, along with a "Rise and shine" from Jack.

David rose and dressed in typical Northwest climbing gear: lightweight cotton shirt, Gortex rainproof windbreaker, multi-pocketed hiking shorts, knee-high thermal socks and state-of-the-art leather boots. When he climbed down the ladder into the kitchen, Jack took one look at him and erupted into raucous laughter.

"Where the hell are you going?" he managed to gasp.

David just stood there, feeling somewhat silly, but glad to see Jack getting such a kick out of his clothes. "Something wrong?"

Jack wiped the tears from his eyes with the back of his hand, then started giggling all over again. "Oh, God," he panted when he finally regained control, "I haven't laughed like that in a long time." He shook his head at David. "This isn't some climbing expedition up Mount Rainier, you greenhorn. Here."

He threw David a pair of baggy overalls. "Strip down to your underwear and put these on. Take off those boots another snicker escaped, "and put on your tennis shoes. You're climbing trees here, not mountains."

"But don't I need more clothing than this to protect me?" David asked.

"No, in fact it's just the opposite. You're gonna peel off the overalls and climb nearly naked. Your skin will help you feel things that may save your life. And you don't want any snake crawlin' between you and your clothes. If you're naked, a snake will just slither on by. Nothin' to worry about, buddy."

David did as he was told and hoped the anxiety, he felt in his gut didn't show. He wasn't crazy about snakes; somehow, he hadn't considered that he might be meeting one on his way up a tree trunk.

While David packed a cooler with food for the day, Jack stowed cages, sacks, and other necessary gear in the back of the car. Then, with a good-bye to Captain Nemo, they set out for the spots they'd found the day before, arriving at the first one just as it was getting light. Jack pointed to a tree, and David stripped to the red skin-tight briefs he posed in during body-building competitions. Hanging a couple gunny sacks around his neck, he was just about to make his ascent when he saw Jack coming around the car with a couple of rifles.

"What are those for?" he asked, frowning. "You're not going to kill anything, are you?"

"Nah. These are just in case I see my best buddy getting his eyes pecked out," explained Jack. "If you're being attacked by a mama bird forty feet up, I don't want to have to rely on my slingshot to scare her away.

David nodded silently, then started up the tree. What have I gotten myself into? he wondered. And then he thought about Rachel and how she was gone from his life forever, and he didn't really care that what he was about to do was dangerous, even life-threatening. Without her, he felt empty, so why not go out in a blaze of glory?

As David climbed, Jack directed him from the ground. Going up was not as easy as Jack had made it out to be. The trees grew so closely together that their branches became hopelessly entangled, and thick vines grew throughout, creating a complicated web of vegetation. By stationing himself several yards away, Jack could help David maneuver around trouble spots.

About thirty feet up David hit pay dirt: two nests with a total of seven babies. He carefully placed the squawking birds into the two sacks and made his way back down.

"Wow!" cried Jack, when he saw David's first haul. "What did I tell ya! Just like pickin' money off trees!"

Flushed with success, David grabbed a couple more sacks and went back up another tree, this one with three nests in it. Each time he came back with several chicks, which Jack would then transfer to the cages. By the end of the day, they had thirty-seven baby birds.

That evening, after making sure all the birds were caged and fed, Jack and David relaxed on the veranda, sipping cold beers. Jack pulled out a hand-rolled cigarette, lit it and sucked in the smoke hungrily, holding the air in his lungs for several seconds. When he exhaled, the sweet smell of marijuana hung in the air.

He looked at David and held out the joint to him.

"Want a hit?" he asked.

David shook his head. "I don't like to take any kind of smoke into my lungs. Thanks anyway."

"I hear ya. This is actually medicinal, to help with the pain of the cancer. But I don't deny that I enjoy it too. And around here, it's the drug of choice. Everybody grows it. Lots of people export it. And a few get killed over it."

David shot Jack an inquisitive look. "Have you had trouble with drug runners?"

"Yeah, there's a few bad asses who have hassled me. But I have protection."

"How do you mean?" asked David, puzzled.

Jack took another hit before answering. "I'll explain it to you, but I don't blame you if you find it hard to believe," he said, exhaling the sweet-smelling smoke. "I mean, this story is straight out of the movies."

"What are you saying? Some local mob bosses have put the finger on you? What'd they do, tell you to pay up or you'll be sorry?" asked David, giving Jack a sarcastic smile.

Jack laughed. "I've got my own mob. They're called The Lost Tribesmen."

Intrigued, David waited as Jack inhaled another dose of "medicine." Then, stubbing out the joint, Jack sat back and began his tale.

"There are several different native tribes in the area, around twenty, I think. Evidently, they have a strict, hierarchical system within each tribe, a pecking order. When somebody rebels against the established hierarchy, they kick him out. It's usually males — guys comin' into their manhood — who cause the trouble. But once in a while they'll banish a young woman, usually for fornicating with the wrong guy."

"Anyway, all these outcasts from the different tribes somehow got together to form their own tribe known as The Lost Tribesmen. They live a stealth like existence no one really knows where they call home. But I think it's near my place, for a number of reasons. When I first

moved here, I started noticing little things that I couldn't explain. I'd go to collect eggs from the chickens and there wouldn't be any — for three days straight. Or I'd dip into the grain bin to feed the oxen only to discover that it was nearly empty, even though I'd just filled it a couple of days before. At first it made me mad, because it's hard enough trying to live out here without people stealing from me."

"Then one morning I walked out onto my porch to find a whole pig, skinned and quartered, just sitting there. Another time it was a string of trout and a bunch of plantains. After talkin' to some of the locals and getting the story on these tribesmen, I realized it must be them, and that they weren't stealing from me but trading with me."

"After that, whenever I had any extra food, I'd leave it out in a certain spot. Finally, they must have decided they could trust me, because one of them approached me when I was out working in the yard. We had sort of a conversation — a little Spanish and a lot of gestures — and he gave me a kind of talisman." Jack pointed to a sculpted piece of bone hanging over his front door. "I gave him a knife from my collection, which I hoped would convey my friendship and trust."

"So how do the drug runners figure into all of this?" asked David.

"I'm gettin' to that. One day some bad lookin' dudes, four of them, roared up my driveway in an old, camouflaged-painted jeep. When I came out to see who they were, they started swearing at me, saying that I stole their land. I guess the plantation had been used to grow marijuana and coca plants in the past, and they aimed to run me off."

"I don't mind tellin' ya, I was scared. These guys were totin' rifles and I had nothin'. I was totally unprepared. I thought they were gonna kill me."

"So, I'm standing there on my porch, wondering what in the hell I'm going to do, when suddenly, one of the guys in the back lets out a scream, grabs his neck, and keels over out of the jeep. He was dead before he hit the ground."

"The other three look around, suddenly terrified. The driver guns the engine, makes a hasty U-turn, and speeds back down the driveway — but not before the guy sittin' shotgun gets picked off too."

"I stood there, stunned, askin' myself, 'What just happened here?' I got down to the post office as quick as I could and put in a call to the local police. I was pretty nervous until they showed up a couple of hours later. 'Drug runners,' the police told me — and they'd been killed by poison darts."

"I've never been hassled since, and I'm sure it's 'cause those lost tribesmen are keepin' an eye on me. As far as I'm concerned, they are welcome to anything of mine they want."

David shook his head appreciatively. "You know, there were times when you were gone that I felt I wasn't alone. I sensed a presence, but I never saw anyone. Now I know they were looking out for me too."

That evening the two men turned in early, eager for the morning to come and, with it, another successful day of birding. They made a good team: Jack with his eye for scoping out nests and spotting the returning parents; David with his stamina and athleticism and gentle way with the babies.

Their days fell into a predictable routine. Up early each morning to either scout locations or go birding, and then returning mid-afternoon to house their new arrivals and take care of the birds already caged. As the number of captive birds grew, their time hunting in the bush dwindled, for the care and feeding of the birds took up more and more of their time.

On one of the mornings they had planned to go hunting, Jack rose slowly, feeling tired and nauseous. David took one look at him and said, "Hey, you don't look so good. Let's skip it today."

Jack shook his head and got out his pot paraphernalia. "A little bit of this will ease the sick-to-my-stomach feeling. Then I'll be okay. Besides, we're close to having our quota, so I don't wanna stop now."

After inhaling hard for a few minutes, Jack brightened visibly, so they ventured out into the jungle. But later that morning, the effects of the drug having worn off, he was once again overcome by queasiness.

At one point he felt so nauseous that he suddenly found himself bent over, upchucking onto the roots of a giant palm. Unfortunately, his timing was poor, for at that moment, a big mama bird was making a beeline for her nest. David, who was just peeking into the tree hole where her nest sat, never saw her coming. His only warning was the sound of an angry squawk just before he felt a searing pain in his ear. Realizing what had happened, he slithered to the ground in record time, blood pouring from the side of his head.

"Jack!" he yelled. "Where the hell are you? I nearly got my head torn off. Jack!"

Jack raised his head feebly. "Here," he croaked, cloaked with undergrowth as he lay on the jungle floor. "Sorry. All of a sudden I just lost it." He saw David's head and sat up quickly. "You're bleeding. God, there's a hell of a lot of blood on you! How bad are you hurt?"

David, who just moments before had been ready to murder his friend, felt his anger evaporate. "My ear's cut, but it's not bad. I'm okay. I was just scared shitless, that's all."

Jack gave a small laugh. "Welcome to the club, my friend. You've just survived the initiation rites."

When they had caught nearly a thousand birds, the maximum capacity for their holding area, Jack and David stopped hunting.

"Time to get them to market and into quarantine, Jack said.

"Where's that?" asked David.

"About ten miles upriver. We'll have to go by barge."

Two days later, Tomás and three men met them at the dock at seven in the morning with two barges. It took the six of them nearly three hours to load over two hundred cages. By then the sun was high and the day was hot. To protect the birds, Jack and David had prepared each cage with a sunscreen, and they spent the next several hours on the river intermittently spraying the cages with water to keep the birds cool.

Finally, late in the day, they arrived at the village where they were able to dock the barges under protective overhangs. It had been a hot and noisy trip, and both Jack and David were tired and hungry. Since the quarantine station was closed until the following morning, Jack and David planned to spend the night on the barges with the birds, protecting their investment.

After checking each cage to make sure the birds were okay, Jack said, "Hey, let's walk into town and get a bite to eat and a beer. I'm buyin'."

They found a dusty Café where they could sit on stools at a bar that looked out onto the town plaza. Jack ordered for them both, and when the owner brought the food to the table, it was plentiful and delicious. The meal began with a soup made from locally grown vegetables, followed by a savory beans-and-rice dish, and ending with a huge platter of tender goat meat in a spicy sauce. Jack, who had smoked some marijuana before they left the barge, shoveled down the food hungrily, including a side dish of his favorite delicacy, hot peppers. His eyes watered, and the sweat began to drip off his brow, but he closed his eyes in ecstasy.

"Umm-hmmm! Nothin' better than hot peppers and cold beer," he said.

David smiled, but said nothing. He had been watching the passers-by, many of them young lovers who walked arm in arm, out for a stroll in the balmy evening air. Except for the day he had arrived in Colombia, when he had hurried through the Bogota airport, this was his first opportunity to mingle with the Colombian people.

He was surprised by the various types of dress he saw. The older people seemed to favor the traditional garments, with most of them wearing the familiar small-brimmed hats and beautifully woven ponchos. But the younger men and women sported western dress, such as shorts, T-shirts, and, of course, Levi's, David noted with a wry smile. Modern fashion had made its way even to this small outpost in the Colombian jungle.

In the center of the plaza was a huge fountain, its stone and brick edifice easily the most attractive piece of architecture in the town. A steady stream of villagers dipped into its waters, carrying jugs filled to the brim back to their log and adobe homes.

As he watched the parade of townspeople pass by the Café, David was struck by their handsome features the high cheekbones, olive skin, and dark hair. The women were especially appealing — a whole country filled with Blacks, he thought. His heart ached with the memory of his own beloved Black, and then a thought struck him. Had he been meant to come here all along? Was the true woman of his dreams here in Colombia, waiting for him to find her?

Later that night, as he fell asleep in his hammock on the barge, he wondered just what God had in store for him. To have given him Rachel, whom he loved more than he could ever describe, and then take her away just as suddenly seemed so cruel. Perhaps all of these events were part of a larger plan, leading up to some kind of outcome that would soothe his broken heart.

With these questions lingering on the periphery of his consciousness, he fell into an uneasy sleep.

The next morning, after seeing to the birds and enjoying a hearty breakfast, Jack and David headed off to the quarantine office, where they were greeted by the owner, Burnie Nelson.

"Jack, good to see you," said Burnie warmly, shaking Jack's hand.

"You, too, you old coot. This is my partner, David Brooks," replied Jack.

Burnie turned his mega-watt smile on David and gave him a firm hand shake. "Glad to hear it. Someone needs to keep Jack in line," he cautioned with a knowing smile.

David immediately liked Burnie, who stood barely five-foot-six and weighed at least 225, though most of that bulk looked like muscle. In his early sixties, Burnie exuded energy, running about the office, handling several tasks at once, and yet able to make his visitors feel welcome and relaxed.

When Jack and Burnie went into an inner office to discuss business, David sat down on a couch in the small waiting room, leaned back, and closed his eyes. As so often happened, Rachel appeared in his mind's eye, and he fantasied about being with her again.

But today the thought of Rachel brought with it an excruciating loneliness. David opened his eyes and looked around the waiting room, searching for something to distract him. Across the room he noticed a rack filled with magazines. One in particular caught his eye, for on its cover was a picture of a woman whose long black hair and olive skin reminded him of the Black. Suddenly, he was weeping uncontrollably, and he escaped to the bathroom where he spent several minutes bathing his face in cold water.

When he had finally composed himself, he returned to the waiting room, where he collided with Jack, who was just emerging from Burnie's office.

"The deal's done!" said Jack, waving a check in the air. "Let's go unload those birds!"

Relieved to have something to do, David followed Jack outside to the barges. With the help of Burnie's men, Jack, David, and Tomás's crew unloaded the birds fairly quickly; then, after farewell handshakes all around, they shoved off down the river. Jack was in high spirits, due in no small part to the generous check he held in his hand.

"Half of this is yours, buddy," he said, passing it over to David.

David took the check and whistled when he saw the number. "That's great, Jack. We're on our way."

He wished he could feel happier about this successful beginning to their venture; perhaps in time he would. Right now, however, it was going to take more than money to fill the hole in his heart.

CHAPTER 14

When Jack and David returned home, they found a visitor waiting for them.

"Keith!" shouted Jack, giving the man a bear hug. "David, meet my old friend, Keith Holmby. We first met when Diane and I were in Africa. He's a pilot, takes people big-game huntin'," explained Jack as David and Keith shook hands. "So, · tell me you just got back from the States."

"I just got back from the States, reported Keith obligingly.

"Did you see Diane?" asked Jack, not bothering to hide his eagerness.

"I did," said Keith, reaching inside his vest pocket, "and she gave me instructions to deliver this to you."

Jack grabbed an envelope out of Keith's hand and retreated to his favorite chair.

"David, get Keith something to drink, okay?"

David and Keith exchanged knowing glances. "Sho' nuff, boss," drawled David, but he said it with a smile.

Keith and David took cold beers out to the veranda where they chatted for half an hour before Jack reappeared.

"She wants to come down here," said Jack. "She's worried about me and she wants to come down right away."

"That's great," said David. "We could use a woman's touch around here." He had met Diane on a number of occasions and had always liked her. Quiet, calm, even a little shy, she provided the perfect counterpoint to Jack's wild ways — and Jack was crazy about her.

Keith spent the night at the homestead. Early the next morning, Jack gave him a lift to the airstrip where he had left his Cessna, and then continued on to the post office, where he put through a call to Diane. After several tries, Jack finally connected, and they made arrangements for her to come down in two weeks.

"Maybe I've already died and gone to heaven," crowed Jack. "Here I am, living in paradise, sitting on a goldmine of a business, with my best buddy and my girl at my side. It doesn't get any better than this!"

For the next several days, Jack and David stayed mostly on the property, making repairs and improvements to the facility. They went birding once or twice, but without much success, for they had depleted the nests within the closest range. Finally, the day came for Diane to arrive. Jack dressed in his finest Colombian shirt, and David drove him to the airstrip. More or less on time, the small, rickety plane that constituted the entire fleet of Aero El Jején dove into view and made its landing.

Jack hurried to the passenger door, reaching it just as it swung open. A petite woman with short-cropped light-brown hair alighted into Jack's waiting arms. There they held each other for several minutes, kissing, talking, and laughing together. Finally, they returned to where David waited by the car.

"Hello, David, it's good to see you" said Diane, giving him a quick hug.

"It's even better to see you," replied David with a smile.
"We can really use you back at the ranch."
"Going to put me to work right away, are you?" laughed Diane. "At least let me get over my jet lag!"
The three returned to the homestead where Diane was suitably impressed.

"David, you did all this?" she exclaimed. "It's unbelievable! When I was last here, this place reminded me of something out of Swiss Family Robinson."
"That's exactly what I thought," David said with a laugh, "but I was too polite to say so."

Jack retrieved cold beers from the fridge, and they adjourned to the deck to chat. David noticed that Diane and Jack were constantly touching each other, exchanging long looks, laughing giddily at the slightest remark. After finishing his beer, he said goodnight, made a sandwich, and retreated to his room for the evening.

Later, as he lay in his bed, a terrible melancholy came over him. He felt both sad and ashamed, for he knew that his depression was brought on by Diane's arrival. Seeing the love and obvious attraction spark between Jack and Diane had reminded him only too vividly of what he had lost.

He had fallen into a nightly ritual of slowly bringing Rachel into his consciousness as he fell asleep. He usually did it little by little, starting with her feet and moving upward, savoring every inch of her body. Sometimes she was nude, and he thrilled at the sight of her tanned, firm, curvaceous body. But more often she was wearing something that complemented her olive complexion and silky black hair. Tonight, when he conjured up The Black in his mind, he was haunted by how he had last seen her   hanging lifeless from a tree, blood dripping down her beautiful face, her vitality gone forever. Try as he might, he could not erase the image from his mind, and he spent a long, sorrowful, sleepless night.

Over the next few days, Diane settled in, making subtle but welcome changes in the men's routine. She took over preparing the meals and showed off her talent for creating something wonderful out of very little. She spent time down in the holding area as well, exhibiting a tenderness and genuine concern for the captive birds that comes from long years of working with animals.

Jack walked around with a perpetual smile on his face, although it was clear that his health was deteriorating. A week after Diane's arrival, he made a suggestion.

"David, we've got to get back out there and get some more birds," he said over the evening meal. "And I just don't feel up to it. I think you and Diane oughta have a go at it."

David had his mouth full of broiled fish, for which he was thankful because he didn't know how to reply. He liked Diane and respected her experience working with animals, but he wasn't sure she would be a good birding partner. If anything should happen to him, he doubted Diane could get him back home safely.

He could feel Diane's eyes on him. He swallowed hard and managed to say, "Uh. . . well, sure... if you think so, Jack."

Jack and Diane both started to giggle. "What's the matter, David?" asked Diane. "Are you afraid to go out into the big bad jungle with me?" "Well, I just thought. . . " started David, but he was cut off by Jack.

"David, haven't I told you how many times this woman saved my life when we were in Africa? She may be a squirt, but she's smart, she's stronger than she looks, and she's very, very resourceful."

David popped a last savory bite in his mouth, set down his knife and fork, and pushed his plate away. "Okay, you're on. But if I come back dead, I'll be pissed!"

After the three of them pored over some topographical maps of the area and decided where to hunt the next day, they turned in. As David lay on his bed, his thoughts, as always, turned to Rachel, and he thought about how he would have loved to share this adventure with her. The glow of a full moon filled his room, and he was staring out his window, marveling at the beauty of the moonscape, when he heard it — a voice that spoke in a loud, clear tone.

"David, don't forget Las Vegas."

David sat up quickly, clutching the bed covers to his chest reflexively. He looked around the room, which was clearly lit by the moonlight, but no one was there. He got up and looked out his window, opening it to make sure there was no one outside on the ground or up on the roof. Satisfied that he was alone, he returned to bed, only to be startled again.

"David, don't forget Las Vegas."

This time he didn't bother to look. He knew the voice he heard belonged to no one. But why he was hearing it — or what it meant — he didn't know.

Four o'clock came early the next morning. David climbed downstairs where he found Diane and Jack nursing cups of coffee.

"It's too early for breakfast," said Diane, "but I'll pack a lot of goodies for the trip."

David and Jack loaded the Range Rover while Diane got the food together. By five they were on the road, David driving and Diane navigating. The first hour wasn't bad, as they travelled roads that were fairly well established. The two of them chatted amiably, mostly about Diane and Jack's adventures in Africa.

"I met Jack when he was down there capturing gorillas for zoos back in the States," Diane explained. "I was there as part of my schooling to be a vet, learning about exotic animals and their care." She took a swig of coffee from her commuter's cup. "I thought he was the most exciting man' I'd ever met. And crazy! He'd do anything, and he has the scars to prove it.

"Did he ever get seriously hurt?" asked David.

"Oh, a few broken bones, but that was about it," said Diane. "He's lucky he wasn't killed." A smile of remembrance crept onto her face. "There was one time when he'd captured this male gorilla and had him sitting in a cage just outside the quarantine station waiting for it to open."

Well, this gorilla was pretty unhappy and started to howl like they do. Before long, a small crowd of' people had gathered around. Jack, ham that he was, decided to put on a show. He walks up to the cage and says, "Hey, pipe down in there," to the gorilla. The gorilla just looks at him and keeps howling. So, Jack pretends to get angry and says, "Do I have to come in there and teach you a lesson?" The cage, which was about eight-by-eight, had a door, and Jack goes over, undoes the lock, and walks in. The gorilla stops his howling and stares at Jack. I guess he didn't know what to do, but it looked like he was pretty mad himself. Jack walks straight up to the gorilla and hauls off and spits right in his eye. 'Take that," he says and calmly walks out of the cage.

"I don't have to tell you that those people were just flabbergasted. They thought Jack was the bravest man they'd ever seen. Turns out Jack knew that in gorilla society, spitting shows dominance, fearlessness. When two gorillas face off, whoever spits first is the winner." Diane laughed out loud at the memory. "God, he was gutsy. Stupid, too, because it could have gone the other way. But that's Jack."

A little after six, David turned off the beaten path and drove as far as he could into the jungle. Then, he and Diane took off on foot, making their way slowly through the vines and underbrush. Since David and Jack had not been in this area at all, they soon spotted some nests and David went to work. By early afternoon, they had nineteen babies.

"One more climb," said David around two.

Diane pointed to a likely looking hole in a tree several yards away. "How about that one? Or is it too high?"

David looked up, guessing that he'd have to climb nearly sixty feet. "I'll let you know when I get up there."

Experienced and intrepid by now, David climbed the tree quickly and easily. At about halfway up, Diane called out, "How are you doing?"

"Piece of cake" came the reply as David continued upward. When he reaches the nest, he carefully looked inside, and then let out a whoop.

"Diane! We hit the jackpot!"

"What? What did you find?"

"They're hyacinths!"

The hyacinth macaws were much more rare than the blue and gold or scarlet macaws that David had captured so far. They were the largest bird of the macaw family, owing in part to their long, flowing tail-feathers, and their coloring was a deep, indigo blue. Although their beaks were strong enough to crush a nut to pieces, their temperament was typically more mellow than their cousins. For all of these reasons, they brought in a much higher price.

This was the first hyacinth nest David had found and he was ecstatic. Instead of putting all four in one bag as he usually did, he gave each of the babies its own bag as an extra precaution and then climbed the along way down very carefully. When he reached the ground, he opens the bags to show Diane. "Four of them," he gloated happily. "They are gorgeous!" said Diane. "I can see why they're so sought after."

Later that afternoon, when David and Diane drove into the courtyard of the homestead, Jack came out to greet them.

"How'd you do?" he asked as he opened Diane's door.

"Not bad," said David offhandedly. "Six blue and golds, nine scarlets, and four hyacinths.' "No shit!" cried Jack. "Let me see!"

David opened the back of the car and Jack carefully unloaded the cages. Carrying the ones with the hyacinths as though they were made of the most fragile crystal, he set them down on a bench and let out a long, low whistle.

"You beautiful babies!" he said to the squawking chicks. Then he turned back to David. "Any more where these came from?"

David looked at Diane. "I don't know, but we'll find out, won't we, partner?"

Diane's eyes crinkled with pleasure. "You bet."

Over the next several days, Diane and David returned to the same area four times, but it wasn't until the first climb of the fourth day that David found another hyacinth nest, this one with only two chicks. Since there were several other nests in nearby trees, David felt certain he would find more of the rare birds.

"At least these nests aren't as high up in the trees as that first one," he said to Diane. "I'll be able to reach more of them in less time."

He eagerly started up his second tree where, about thirty feet up he could see a likely looking hole just below where the tree trunk split into a Y. As he slowly peeked inside, he was greeted by a welcome sight: three baby hyacinths with their mouths open, waiting for dinner.

And then he saw something else — something that made his heart stop: the beady and malevolent eyes of a snake. It was sitting in the crook of the tree trunk just above him, its long torso coiled around a branch, its gaze fixed on David. Just by the size and shape of the snake's head, he could tell it was a boa constrictor, a large, mature, angry boa constrictor. And it had David in its sights.

Although a boa kills its prey by squeezing them to death, David knew that, when threatened, a boa would strike. He did not move for several minutes, not just because he was paralyzed with fright, but because he knew not to move until he had a plan. He frantically racked his brain for a way to intimidate the snake, so he could make his escape, but the only thing that came to mind was Diane's story of Jack and the gorilla.

His arms were aching, and he knew he would have to make a move soon. What the hell, thought David, I'll give spitting a try:

David cleared his throat and tossed a line of spittle that hit the snake right on its nose. The snake didn't move, nor did it take his gaze away from David. Once again, David cleared his throat and spit right at the snake, this time hitting him in the eye. Moving with lightning speed, the snake struck at David with its jaws open, ready to kill.

The snake connected with David's neck, where its teeth sunk into his flesh. But it had hit David so hard that the sheer force of the attack made the snake lose its lethal grip. David was knocked backwards out of the tree; then he plummeted down to the ground in two seconds flat, hitting a couple of branches on the way which helped to slow his fall.

He lay there for quite a while, not sure just how badly he was hurt.

"David!" He could hear Diane's voice wafting through the trees, calm but alarmed. "David, if you can hear me, please answer!

David opened his mouth to reply but nothing came out. Then he realized that he wasn't breathing and suddenly everything went black.

" . . .okay?" David could hear a woman speaking, but his mind flashed back to Las Vegas where Dick Sloane had awakened him with the same words. Where was he? Where was Rachel? Was she okay?

"You took quite a fall. Don't move until I check you out," said the woman's voice. That was okay with David; he didn't feel like doing anything.

He felt the gentle pressure of confident hands as they moved around his body.

"David, this is Diane. Can you hear me?' A weak "yes" passed his lips.

"I'm going to touch your legs and arms, and I want you to tell me if you can feel it."

God, it's all I can do to maintain consciousness, thought David. But he managed to answer in the affirmative to all of Diane's probes.

'Can you tell me where it hurts?" asked Diane.

"Everywhere," whispered David.

"Okay. Just lie still. I'll be back in a few minutes.

Twenty minutes later she returned, carrying a primitive but sturdy homemade stretcher behind her. She pulled David onto it, then dragged him back to the car where she loaded him through the rear door. Once he was as comfortable as he could be, she climbed behind the wheel.

"Now let's hope I can find our way back home," she muttered to herself.

The drive back to Jack's was a long and tedious one. Diane took more than one wrong turn and she drove slowly to minimize the effect of the bumpy roads on David's bruised body. It was nearing dark when she finally pulled into the courtyard of the homestead.

"Hey!' Jack called to Diane from the veranda. "I was starting to worry about you two." Then he noticed that David was lying in the rear of the car rather than sitting in the passenger's seat. "Oh, God, what happened?"

"David took quite a tumble," replied Diane as she walked to the back of the car and opened the rear door. "Help me get him inside."

By this time David felt well enough to be upright, but he couldn't put any weight on one leg. Diane and Jack managed to get him into the house and onto the sofa.

"You have a doctor nearby who'll make a house call?" asked Diane.

"Yeah," said Jack. "You stay with David and I'll run down to the post office and give him a call."

Two hours later, Dr. Sojero finished his examination of David.

"Looks like a dislocated shoulder, a sprained ankle, and a nasty snake bite — not to mention a few bruises. I'd say you are very lucky," he pronounced.

"Yeah," said David with a rueful smile. "That's me
— lucky."

"Well, you will feel a whole lot better in a few days." The doctor fixed David with his sternest glare. "Listen to me. If you want to get better, stay off your feet." David nodded weakly.

After the doctor left, Diane made the couch into a bed for David and Jack fixed a late-night snack. All the while, Captain Nemo hovered around David, bringing out his prized possessions — band aids — to share with him.

As they sat munching sandwiches and dill pickles, Jack asked David what happened.

"I met a boa constrictor, thirty feet up in a tree," replied David.

"You're kidding!" said Jack, shaking his head in disbelief.

"People don't usually walk away from a boa attack."

"Well, I didn't exactly walk away. Thanks, by the way," he said to Diane.

"I told ya she could do the job," said Jack proudly. "How'd it happens?"

David described the encounter, explaining how he had spit in the snake's face.

"You did what?" cried Jack, incredulous.

"I thought if it worked with gorillas, it might work with snakes, " replied David.

Both Jack and Diane stared at David, speechless. Then they dissolved into gales of laughter, so long and so hearty that tears spilled down their cheeks. Even Captain Nemo seemed to think the story funny, jumping around the room and shrieking happily.

It was several minutes before the hilarity subsided. Jack rubbed the tears from his eyes and cast an affectionate smile toward David. "You know, David, now that I think about it, that spitting" — he chuckled again, shaking his head — your spitting at that snake just may have saved your life."

"How so?" asked Diane.

"The way I figure it, that snake was probably so pissed off that it struck David too hard for its teeth to sink into his neck, which would have killed him. Instead, the blow knocked him out of the tree where he fell to safety."

David nodded but said nothing. Tired and sore, he opened the bottle of pain pills left by the doctor and washed a couple down with a glass of iced tea. Then, gingerly, he lay back on the couch to slowly sink into oblivion.

David followed the doctor's advice and spent the next two weeks taking it easy. During that time, Diane and Jack went back to Bogota to visit Jack's doctors and take a minivacation. When David picked them up on their return, he could tell by their subdued mood that things had not gone well.

"Well, it appears that I'm on my way out," said Jack without any preliminaries. "The cancer has spread, and they can't help me anymore.

David kept quiet for a few moments, letting the meaning of the words sink in before he spoke. "We each have our time, and I guess all we can do is trust in God that it's the right time," he said slowly, thinking of Rachel. "Although we can't change our fate, we can make the most of the time we have right now."

"Amen to that," said Jack, and then he brightened. "Let's go home and have a few beers!"

The next several weeks went quickly, with David and Diane back to birding and Jack taking care of things at home. While Diane and Jack were in Bogota, David had designed himself a helmet of sorts, something to protect his head, neck, and chest from future attacks from snakes. He felt more confident returning to the spot where the boa had attacked him, although he didn't encounter any others. Instead, just as he had predicted, he found many more hyacinth, macaws in that same area, so that when they were ready to visit the quarantine again, almost one hundred of their birds were these precious parrots.

Preparations for going to quarantine were much like the time before. Tomás arrived early in the morning and he and his crew helped to load the cages onto the barges. At one-point David drew him aside and asked that he clear a spot near the bow of the first barge. There David installed Jack's favorite leather recliner, complete with fishing pole holders and accompanied by a portable CD player that blared Pink Floyd and the Blues Brothers, Jack's favorite music.

"What's all this?" asked Jack when he saw David's handiwork.
"Hey, I just thought we'd go in style this time," he said.
"Whooeee!" cried Jack, plopping down in the chair.
"Barkeep, bring me a beer!" he shouted with mock imperiousness. David opened the chair-side cooler and shoved a cold one in his hand.

Once again, the journey took most of the day. When they arrived in port in the late afternoon, Tomás deftly guided the barges under the cover of the metal cabanas where they would stay until morning.

Diane, Jack, and David walked into town for a relaxing evening meal at the same little restaurant the men had been to before. Again, they chose a table that allowed them to watch the passers-by stroll along the avenue. But this time the beautiful dark-haired woman and affectionate young lovers did not send David into a reflective and despondent mood. To the contrary, he felt oddly alert, almost wired, as if all his nerves were standing at attention. On a subconscious level his senses were reacting to some stimulus, but what it was he did not know. He felt in his gut, however, that something was about to happen.

After dinner, Jack and Diane walked up the street to a little motel where they planned to stay the night. David returned to once again sleep in a hammock on board one of the barges; a member of

Tomás's crew had agreed to spend the night on the other. Although David was exhausted from the trip, he found it hard to fall asleep with his adrenaline coursing so violently through his body. He got little rest that night.

The next morning after breakfast, David, Diane, and Jack made their way to the quarantine office. As before, Burnie welcomed them warmly.

"And who is this?" he asked, taking Diane's hand in both

"This is the love of my life," said Jack, putting his arm around Diane. "Diane O'Keefe, Burnie Nelson."

"Delighted," smiled Burnie. "Please, come inside my office."

Jack and Diane followed Burnie into the cramped and cluttered office. "Back in a few," said Jack to David, unless you wanna come along."

David shook his head. "No, thanks. I'll wait."

He took a seat on the couch in the waiting room and, once again his gaze fell on the revolving magazine rack against the far wall. Suddenly, every hair on his body stood up straight as a jolt like an electric shock ripped through his body. He jumped to his feet and fairly flew across the room to the rack, spinning it around until he found what he was looking for: the dog-eared magazine he had seen before that featured a stunning raven-haired woman on its cover. It was Rachel.

CHAPTER 15

Rachel felt herself floating, engulfed in warmth and light. Where was she? she wondered. She was drifting, like a balloon that had escaped its tether, not knowing where she was going nor caring. A bright glow in the distance beckoned to her and she felt herself being drawn toward it, content to let it pull her into its comforting aura. But... no, something was not right. A nagging doubt cast its shadow, dimming the power of the light. Rachel realized she couldn't go, not yet.

The next thing she remembered was awaking in a sterile white room. Anxious faces peered down at her and she could feel the uncomfortable hardness of plastic in her nose and mouth.

"She's coming to," she heard a woman say.

A figure almost completely covered in white bent over her.

"Miss Black, can you hear me?" he asked. "Don't try to move. If you can understand me, just blink your eyes to answer yes."

Rachel stared at him for a long moment, then slowly blinked her eyes.

"Good!" the man said, and she felt the pressure of his hand squeezing her arm encouragingly. "You were in a serious auto accident and the paramedics brought you here, to St. Elizabeth's.

I'm Dr. Hellier, and I've performed some surgery on you. That's why you've got all these tubes sticking out of you."

He paused to see if there was any recognition in Rachel's eyes of what he was telling her. She appeared to be alert and focused on his words.

"The good news is that you came through the surgery   with flying colors. Although it will take a while, you should recover fully."

Rachel closed her eyes, remembering the warmth and the light she had felt — just moments ago it seemed. She must have been close to death, but she was going to live, to be all right. Still she was terribly distressed, feeling an urgent need to tell this man something very important, but exactly what it was she did not know. Instead, she closed her eyes and succumbed to an overwhelming exhaustion.

Two days later Rachel was well enough to breathe on her own, and the tubes from her mouth and nose were extracted. Her parents, who already had visited her several times, came by just as the nurse was leaving.

"Rachel!" cried her mom, bending down to give her daughter a kiss. "You look much better without all those things sticking out of you. Can you talk?"

Rachel didn't know herself. "Yes," came the weak, squeaky reply.

"Honey, you don't need to say anything yet, said her dad. "Just relax. We're taking care of everything, so you don't have to worry."

Although Rachel had been disoriented when she first came to the hospital, she had had two days to regain her bearings. What had been troubling her was now clear in her mind.

"Where's David?" she whispered. "Have you seen him?"

Walter and Lydia exchanged glances. "No," replied her dad, surprised. "Haven't you?"

Rachel blinked back tears. "I don't think anyone's been to see me but you," she croaked, and the tears spilled onto her cheeks.

"Oh, honey," soothed her mom, taking Rachel's hand. "Don't worry. He's probably been here, and you didn't know it. Or maybe they wouldn't let him in because he's not a member of the family. You two weren't married yet, so technically they could have kept him out."

Rachel thought about this and decided it was possible. She just couldn't believe that David had deserted her, not now.

But as the days went by, still no David appeared. One nurse in the intensive care unit, Janet, took a special interest in Rachel, intrigued by this beautiful woman who became more depressed and listless each day.

"It's natural to feel blue after an accident such as yours," Janet said once morning as she changed Rachel's bed. "Your body had a severe physical and emotional shock. Depression is a common reaction.

Rachel looked down at her hands, which were covered with scratches. "It's not the accident that's depressing me."

With a little prompting from Janet, Rachel spilled the story about the David, from how they first met to their wedding plans. As she finished the tale, Rachel dissolved into sobs. "Where could he be?" she cried. "Why isn't he by my side?"

Janet put an arm around her. "If all you say is true, I can't believe he would leave you," she said comfortingly. "Don't worry. We'll find him."

When Rachel was moved out of intensive care and into a regular hospital room, Janet asked to be temporarily reassigned so she could remain Rachel's primary caregiver. In the following days, she quizzed Rachel constantly about David: Who were his friends? What business was he in? Where had he lived? Janet's keen interest and determination gave Rachel hope, and she racked her brain for every detail she could remember about David.

One afternoon Janet, dressed in her street clothes, strode into her patient's room, a confident bounce to her step.

Rachel, who had been working a crossword puzzle, looked up in surprise. "Janet, hi! I thought it was your day off."
"It is. And guess what I've been doing!" Before Rachel could say anything, Janet answered for her. "Detective work! I went down to the sheriff's department and found the officer who was first called to the scene of the accident!"

Rachel looked at Janet, not understanding the significance of this.
"Rachel," continued Janet, her excitement palpable,
"that officer told me there was a man at the scene, someone who tried to come down the embankment to see you."
Rachel sat up straight. "What did he look like?"

Janet shook her head. "The officer doesn't remember that, but he did recall the kind of car he was driving." Janet paused for dramatic effect. "It was a dark blue BMW!" "David!" shrieked Rachel.

"That's not all," said Janet. "This officer said the man was terribly distraught, causing a scene and assaulting officers, trying to get down to you. But the officer I talked to stopped him cold because he told him you were dead."

Rachel stared at Janet, her eyes wide, her mouth gaping. "Why would he do that?"

"Because for a while they couldn't find a pulse on you. They had you covered like a corpse when David arrived."

A slow smile crept onto Rachel's face, the first real smile Janet had seen since she had first met Rachel.

"David thinks I'm dead!"

"I know! Isn't it wonderful?" cried Janet, and the two women fell into each other's arms, laughing and crying.

Finally, Rachel drew back, wiping her eyes. "So, he hasn't left me," she whispered. "I knew it, in my heart, I just knew something had happened."

"Now, all we have to do is find him," said Janet. "How hard can that be?"

Over the. next several days, Rachel and Janet tried to come up with a plan to locate David. They had already checked every place they could think of, with no luck. Rachel hadn't yet met any of David's friends, and since he had planned on moving in with her, his forwarding address was of no help. No one at the Westside Gym knew where he had gone, only that he hadn't been in for a couple of weeks.

The only positive note during that time came from Janet, who remained determined in her search and optimistic that everything would turn, out all right. One morning when she came to visit

Rachel, she had a skinny young man in tow. His wire-rimmed glasses and sparse goatee gave him a sheepish look, like a schoolboy caught out of class. Janet introduced him to Rachel.

"This is Andrew Ashby," she said. "He's a writer for the magazine Modern Medicine, and he is very interested in your story."

The young man hung back a bit, as though embarrassed to be in the presence of such an attractive woman who wore nothing but a hospital gown. Rachel looked at Janet with some apprehension, not sure exactly what to say.

Picking up on Rachel's anxiety, Janet quickly went on. "What interested Andrew initially was the fact that you were pronounced dead at the scene," she said. "I've given him all the gory details how a branch of the tree pierced your body but missed the organs, how you had no discernible pulse, how the officer covered your body with
a blanket as though you were dead." She gave the young man a quick look, hoping he would jump in and continue the explanation, but he was gazing at the foot of Rachel's bed, obviously still very uncomfortable. "When I started talking about David and how he was missing, Andrew thought that would lend a wonderful human-interest angle to his story."

Rachel looked at the young man with new interest. Giving him a smile that would melt an iceberg, she said, "If you could help me find him, I would be so appreciative. It would mean the world to me."

At this Andrew raised his gaze to meet Rachel's, and he seemed to relax. Pulling up an orange vinyl chair, he sat down, took out a notebook, and clicked open his pen.

"Okay," he said with a shy smile, "let's get started."

For the next two and a half hours, Andrew interviewed Rachel, draining her of every bit of information she had within her. At the end of the session, he put away his notebook and pen and stood awkwardly.

"I can't promise you anything," he said, looking down at his shoes, "but the story will probably be out in the next issue, about four weeks from now." Somehow, he brought himself to look her straight in the eye. "I hope it helps you find him."

Rachel put her hand to clasp his. All she said was "Thank you."

Finally, the day came for Rachel to check out of the hospital. She sat on the edge of her bed, depressed and defeated, as she waited for her parents to come and pick her up.

"I'm never going to find him," she lamented to Janet, who was waiting with her. "Where could he have gone? He's just disappeared."

"Don't give up," said Janet, encouragingly. "Love like yours doesn't come along very often. You'll find each other, I just know it."

A few minutes later, Walter and Lydia walked in. Seeing Rachel's face, Walter asked, "Baby, what's wrong? Are you in pain?"

Rachel gave him a rueful smile. "You could say that."

Lydia sat down next to her. "You haven't found David yet, have you?" she asked softly, putting an arm around her daughter.

Rachel shook her head. "We fell in love so fast, there's still a lot I don't know about him. I have no idea where to look."

Walter gazed down at his daughter whom he loved more than anything in the world. "Hell, if you can't find him, we'll just have to make him find you.

Rachel, Lydia, and Janet all looked up at him with puzzled faces. "What do you mean?" asked Rachel.

"Well, I've got more money than God, having won that lottery. Let's just use that. We'll put on a big ad campaign, all across Washington maybe even the whole country — whatever it takes to let him know that you are alive and waiting for him."

Rachel jumped up and threw her arms around her dad's neck. "What a great idea!" she cried and gave her father a grateful hug. "Dad, you are the best!"

"Look out, Lion, we're going to hunt you down!" cried Janet, pumping her fist in the air, and, in spite of herself, Rachel laughed along with everyone else.

The following Monday found Walter, Lydia, and Rachel in the offices of Didereaux and Howe, Seattle's most prestigious public relations firm, consulting with advertising guru Robert Didereaux himself.

"I've conducted a lot of interesting ad campaigns over the years," he told them, "but I think yours will be the most intriguing one of them all."

"Do you think you can help us?" asked Rachel anxiously.

Bob Didereaux smiled. "Your David would have to be deaf, dumb, and blind not to get your message. I can promise you that."

Thus, began an intense advertising campaign that included billboards in all fifty states, nationwide TV commercials, radio spots, banners on buses, and thousands of flyers inserted in countless publications. Because they didn't want every nut in the country calling to say he was the man they were looking for, Rachel and Janet came up with a tagline that would make sense only to David: The Black Is Alive — Lion Come Home.

A month passed without any word from David, leaving Rachel even more depressed than before. It was difficult for her to believe that he hadn't seen or heard something, yet he still had not contacted her. Even though she was staying with her parents, all phone calls to her home were forwarded there. If David had called, he would have reached her.

One evening, as Rachel lay on her bed staring at the ceiling, she thought about the first few hours after her accident when she had felt the warmth and comfort of the beckoning light. Now she wished she had let the light take her. If she had known she was coming back to a life without David, she would simply have allowed herself to drift away.

A knock at her door interrupted her melancholy daydream.

"Rachel?" Walter's voice came through the door. "Rachel, can I come in?" At the sound of her faint "yes, he opened the door, the corners of his mouth fighting a losing battle with a smile. "Rachel, how would you like to go on TV?"

"I've already been on TV," said Rachel, "and he still hasn't called."

"No, I don't mean in another commercial like the ones Didereaux and Howe had you do. I mean on a TV show   a really popular, widely watched TV show."

Rachel looked at him hopefully. "You mean like Town Meeting?" she asked, citing a locally produced TV talk show.

"No, something more like... Oprah!" announced Walter with a big grin.

"Oh my God! Are you kidding?" screamed Rachel.

"Next Friday, in Chicago. It's all set up."

Rachel shook her head, speechless. What an opportunity! Even if David didn't see it, surely someone who knew him and his whereabouts would be watching.

And then if he didn't call, she would know it was because he didn't want to.

"I'll start packing," said Rachel.

The theme for the show on which Rachel appeared focused on people who had lost and then found each other. One guest was a woman who recently had been reunited with the son she had given up for adoption twenty-five years earlier. Another man and woman were high school sweethearts who had lost touch when the man went off to fight in World War Il, only to find each other again in their golden years. A particularly heart-wrenching story was told by a father who appeared with his eleven-year-old daughter. She had been spirited away by his ex-wife at age three, and it had taken him eight years to track her down.

Oprah saved Rachel's story for last, because Rachel had not yet found the person she was looking for.

"Ladies and gentlemen," Oprah began, "our last guest is a woman who has gained some notoriety in the past few weeks. You all know her as the Black." A murmur went up from the crowd.

"Unless you've been living in a cave," continued Oprah, "you have seen signs or heard commercials that say the Black is alive and well and for the Lion to come home. Y'all wonder what that was about?"

The crowd came to life, applauding wildly to show their interest.

"Well, meet Rachel, also known as the Black, a name given her by her lover, the Lion, because, as you can see, she has all that beautiful dark hair. She has quite a story to tell." Oprah turned to Rachel, who sat nervously in her overstuffed chair. "Rachel, why don't you just start at the beginning."

For the next ten minutes, Rachel told the story of the Lion and the Black, with Oprah asking her a question here and there. When she finished, the studio audience was still, mesmerized by her tale. Oprah turned to the cameras.

"Lion, honey, if you are out there, we're here to tell you that your woman is fine, and she is waiting for you. So, give her a call!"

After the show, Oprah gave Rachel a big hug. "I bet he's on the phone calling you right now," she said.

As soon as Rachel returned to the hotel, she called home, as she did just about every hour on the hour until their plane departed the next day. But the answer Lydia gave her was always the same: David had not called.

On her return to her parents' house, Rachel retired to her room where she remained for the next several days. Occasionally her mom or dad would knock lightly, asking to come in and chat with her. Rachel always assented, but she seemed miles away, lost in her own private pain.

They began to worry about her, wondering whether she might do something drastic.

Their fears were not unfounded. After hours and hours of thinking about what had happened, Rachel had begun to consider a new possibility, a tragic scenario which, the more she thought about it, the more she believed could be true.

She kept replaying Bob Didereaux's words in her head: "Your David would have to be deaf, dumb, and blind not to get your message."

He had forgotten to mention dead. What if, in the classic tradition of Romeo and Juliet, David, on learning of Rachel's "death," had taken his own life? It was the only explanation that made sense to her. She knew in her heart that David had been completely committed to her. He was the one who had pursued her, who had made it clear to her that he loved her more than life itself. It made no sense that he would suddenly abandon her — unless he was convinced that she was dead, and he had made plans to join her.

With this thought in mind, Rachel contemplated her own death. She had fought death before, thinking she couldn't leave David behind. But, evidently, she had made the wrong choice. If they were to be together, it seemed that it would not be in this dimension, but in the next.

One evening she lay on her bed, thinking about whether she would have the courage to take her own life. Such thoughts were alien to her — she was a fighter, and suicide seemed like a quitter's way out. But if David had had the strength to do it, couldn't she?

David. . . who respected and took care of his physical self-more than anyone she knew. David. . . who never missed taking his vitamins, who drank endless protein drinks, who worked out at the gym religiously. Would he really do anything to harm that beautiful body, to shut it down permanently?

Slowly, a sensation began to ripple through her body a fiery, pulsating, tingly sensation like nothing she had ever felt before. She sat up and looked into the mirror. Her face was flushed, and she could feel that all of her senses were heightened. What is going on? she asked herself. Is this my body's way of protesting its possible demise?

Suddenly she was engulfed by thoughts of David — the way he smiled, the smell of his hair, the sweet and loving touch of his hands on her body. It was as if he were in her room.

Downstairs, she heard the phone ring, and she knew. Her Lion was about to come home.

CHAPTER 16

When David realized it was Rachel's picture on the cover of Modern Medicine, he let out a yell that brought Jack and Diane scrambling out of Burnie's office.

"David!" cried Jack. "What's wrong? What happened?" David stood completely still. He didn't answer for several seconds but just stared at the magazine in his hands. Then he turned and shoved the magazine at Jack.

"She's alive," he whispered, and then shouted, "She's alive! My God! She's alive!"

David grabbed Diane in a crushing hug, lifting her up and twirling her around the room. Jack looked down at the magazine that displayed the beautiful dark-haired woman on its cover. The caption below the photo read "Left for Dead."

"This is Rachel?" asked Jack in disbelief.

David, who was still dancing around the tiny waiting room with Diane in his grasp, yelled, "That's Rachel! My

Black Beauty! Can you believe it? She's not dead after all!" He dropped a dizzy Dianne on the couch and snatched the magazine unceremoniously out of Jack's hands.

"There must be a story in here about it," he said, thumbing through the pages frantically until he found a picture of the battered Jaguar. "Look! That's her car! And that's her being loaded into the ambulance! Oh, God! Why did they tell me she was dead?"

Jack took the magazine back and quickly scanned the copy to find out what had happened. "Because they thought she was dead until an alert paramedic found a pulse. Holy shit! Look at this picture. She's got a branch sticking through her body! And she lived!"

Having recovered her equilibrium, Diane came over and took the magazine from Jack, who grabbed his friend in a warm embrace.

"I am so happy for you, buddy. Goddammit, your life always did play like some kind of action movie! Unbelievable!"

"Listen to this!" interrupted Diane excitedly, and then read from the article." "As this magazine goes to press, Miss Black plans to launch a nationwide advertising campaign to let Mr. Brooks, wherever he is, know that she is alive and well and waiting for him to come home.

"David, I remember seeing those ads, but they didn't have your picture. I had no idea you were the Lion!"

By this time, Burnie had come out of the office to see what all the commotion was about. Once he understood what had happened, he beamed at David with genuine delight.

"Congratulations, my friend!" he exclaimed, grabbing David's hand and pumping it excitedly. "And to think you found her right here in my little waiting room!

"Burnie, what the hell are you doing with Modern Medicine, anyway?" asked Jack, a suspicious grin on his face. "You're no doctor."

"No, but my brother-in-law is. All these magazines are from his waiting room at the clinic. He kindly gives them to me when he is through with them." Turning to David again, he said, "You will want to call your young woman right away. Please, come into my office. It would be my pleasure to be a part of this fantastic story."

Gratefully, David followed Burnie into the small office dominated by a huge mahogany desk. Burnie picked up the phone and spoke in Spanish to a succession of operators. Finally, he handed the phone to David.

"Just tell her the number you want, and she will get it for you," he said.

Trembling, David recited Rachel's phone number. He listened to the clicks and whirs as the number connected and then transferred to Walter and Lydia's phone.

"Hello?" he heard a man's voice answer.

Without any explanation, David said, "I'm calling for Rachel."

A few seconds later he heard the voice he thought he'd never hear again. It was soft and wondering as it whispered, "Is it you?"

"It's me."

The next thing David heard was an ear-piercing shriek followed by a loud thump as the phone hits the floor.

The first few minutes of David and Rachel's conversation were spent in happy confusion as they both talked at once, words bubbling out of their mouths seemingly of their own accord as each one confessed how miserable they had been without the other.

Finally, after their initial frenzy abated, they got down to the details of getting David home as quickly as possible. It was decided that he would catch the first plane home he could and have a travel agent fax her the particulars of his arrival.

"And I want to get married as soon as we can,' insisted David. "I don't ever want to take a chance on losing you again.

"Don't worry," laughed Rachel. "I'm not letting you get away this time."

"I love you more than ever," said David. "I can't wait until I have you in my arms again."

Although David was tempted to leave for Bogota immediately, he knew that doing so would make things difficult for Jack, who could barely get around on his own any more. So, he returned to the homestead with the barges, where he unloaded the cages and set them up for the next influx of birds.

That evening, over dinner, Jack brought up the subject himself.

"I know you need to go, buddy. And I'm happy for you. But, just remember, we want you here. I hope that once things settle down, you and Rachel will talk about comin' down here and being our partners in this operation. Shit, I'm not gonna be around forever, you know. Try to get back down here as soon as you can so we can cash in on the market. Two or three more hauls would give you a tidy little nest egg for whatever you and Rachel wanted to do."

David lifted his wine glass to Jack and Diane. "There's no one I'd rather have as partners. I promise that we will give it our sincere consideration — but not until after our honeymoon, which I plan to make a long one!"

The next afternoon, David, Jack, and Diane waited on the primitive runway as Pablo eased his rattletrap plane into a perfect three-point landing. At the homestead earlier, David had said goodbye to Captain Nemo, who seemed distraught at his departure. The monkey squawked and screeched in distress, even bringing out packages of band aids which he presented to David as an enticement to get him to stay.

"You are a silly little bugger," said David as he rubbed the Captain's head. "I'll miss you too."

Before David climbed into the plane, he gave both Diane and Jack a big hug. "Please, take care," he said.

"Oh, I will," said Jack dismissively with a wave of his hand. "Just try to get back on down here before I croak, will ya? I'd like to meet this fabulous babe."

Upon landing back in the Bogota airport, David made his way to the El Jején check-in counter where he asked Hector to direct him to a travel agent.

"But I can help you right here, senior," Hector replied with a smile. "As you can see, I have a computer. I will find you the best flight for the best price."

The first flight David could get would depart early the next morning for Miami. After a five-hour layover there, he would board a charter flight that would fly nonstop to Seattle.

Since David had an evening to kill, and he had seen nothing of Bogota when he arrived, he decided to play the role of tourist. He jumped into a cab just outside baggage claim and asked the driver to take him to a nice hotel. After checking in, he gave a copy of his flight itinerary to the hotel manager.

"Can you fax this to the States for me?" he asked, slipping the manager a generous tip.

"Sí, señor, right away," replied the man with a smile.

After freshening up in his room, David headed down to the fern-filled lobby and out into the lingering daylight to take a walk along the boulevard. The sidewalks were full of people, some bustling along quickly as they hurried home to dinner, others strolling languidly as they idly window-shopped. David found a corner cafe where he could dine on the patio and drink in the local color. He thought back to the last time he had been in this city, beset by such deep misery that he thought he would never find his way out. How different he felt on this visit. Tonight, he was filled with indescribable joy and a serenity that comes from knowing that all is right with the world. Soon, he would be with his Black.

The next morning, David checked in at the Lan-Chile Airlines ticket counter well before his flight. With nearly two hours to wait until take-off, he wandered around the airport, anxious and excited, needing to walk off some of his energy. He bought a couple magazines for the flight, but once on board, he was too keyed up to read. Instead, he closed his eyes and fantasized about his reunion with Rachel.

In Miami, after clearing customs and immigration, David hailed a cab and directed its driver to take him to the nearest gym. There he went through most of his regular exercise regimen, the first real workout he'd had since the day of Rachel's accident. After a rubdown and a shower, he again whistled for a taxi, this time instructing the cabby to take him to a barber shop.

At Julien's For Men, an elderly barber gave David's hair a trim and carefully shaved the overgrown stubble. Then, as he pulled a steaming towel from David's face, he peered over his spectacles for a closer look.

"You look familiar," he said slowly, trying to place the face. "Hey, ain't you that lion guy? The one that dame's been lookin' all over for?"

David blushed. "Well, I..."

The older man didn't wait for David to finish. "Hey, Ernie, come here," he yelled to his partner. "This is that guy, the Lion, the one whose face was all over those magazines a couple of weeks ago."

Another ancient man shuffled over and inspected David. "Yeah, you're the one. Does she know where you are?" Then, suddenly, his wrinkled face brightened as a thought occurred to him. "Hey, maybe there's a reward!" David rose out of the chair hastily. "Actually, I'm on my way home to her right now," he said, pulling some bills out of his pocket and handing them to the barber. "Thanks. Keep the change."

He hurried out of the shop, wondering how they had known what he looked like. He thought Diane had said that Rachel hadn't used his picture. Shrugging it off, he flagged down another taxi, this time asking to be taken to the best clothiers in town.

"Good afternoon. My name is James," a salesman greeted him as David entered the store. He was a quite a bit younger than David, sharply dressed and fresh faced. "How can I help you today?"

David didn't waste any time. "I've got exactly forty-five minutes and two grands to spend. I want jacket and slacks, shirt and tie, socks and shoes. Not too formal — kind of casual but classic. And I only want to look at the best-quality stuff. Think you can do it?"

The man broke out into a big smile. "You bet! Follow me."

As David tried on slacks, James cast a sideways glance at him, trying to size up David without being rude. Finally, he asked, "Have we met before?"

"I don't think so," replied David, looking over his shoulder at his rear-view image in the three-way mirror.

"This is my first time in Miami."

But I'm sure I've seen your face. Are you an actor, or a model maybe?"

"Nope, just a guy on his way home to Seattle to — " "You're the Lion!" James snapped his fingers and pointed at David. "Of course! I've seen your picture in the paper, and in Time magazine too."

David looked at him in disbelief. "You're kidding. Why would my picture be in Time?"

James laughed and shook his head. "Man, you don't know what's been going on! The whole country's been buzzing about the Lion. First there were these mysterious ads "Lion come home, the Black's alive" or something like that. No one knew what the heck they all were about. Then the woman —Rachel."

"Yeah, Rachel, went on Oprah, and the media got a hold of the story, and suddenly your picture was everywhere."

David stared at his reflection in the mirror in wonder. What was he coming home to?

An hour later David walked out of the shop looking as though he were heading for a photo shoot for GQ magazine. With him was James, who had insisted on driving David to the airport himself.

"Hey, I'm happy to do it," he said with a smile. "It's just a thrill to meet you, to be a bit player in this great love story. And, I'll have a great tale to tell my friends!"

David made it back to the airport just as they were calling for passengers to board the chartered flight. He stowed his carry-on in an overhead compartment and took his aisle seat in the fifteenth row. Before long, he noticed a young woman sitting two rows up and across the aisle from him. She seemed to be staring at him.

David took out a magazine and tried to read, but he could feel the woman's eyes on him. Once the plane had taken off and the seatbelt sign had been extinguished, the young woman made her way back to David. "Excuse me," she said shyly.

When David looked up, he met the earnest gaze of a woman in her early twenties whose wholesome face was framed by carrot-colored ringlets. "I hope you won't think I'm rude, but I couldn't help noticing you." She paused as if unsure as to whether she should continue.

David smiled, putting her at ease. "It's just that. . . well, you look just like the Lion." She hesitated again. "Are you? The Lion, I mean?" David grinned broadly. He looked up the aisle and could now see several other faces peering back at him.
"Yes, I guess I am."

The woman let out a little scream and then clapped her hand over her mouth, embarrassed. She turned back to her companion, another woman about the same age who had her head stuck out into the aisle, straining to hear what they were saying.

"It is!" cried the first woman in an excited whisper. Then she turned back to David and shoved a pen and paper in his hands. "Could I have your autograph?"

Before long, it seemed as though the whole plane knew who David was. A stewardess came back to talk to him, asking if he would mind sharing his story with the rest of the passengers. David, more amused than annoyed by all the attention, dutifully explained where he had been and where he was going. A few minutes later, the stewardess came on the intercom.

"Ladies and gentlemen, as you may have guessed, we have a celebrity on board. Most of you have probably seen those unusual ads on TV or read the story in Time about a beautiful young woman searching for her Lion. For you who don't know the story, it is quite remarkable. The young woman had been in a terrible car accident and was pronounced dead at the scene. When her fiancé, the Lion, was given the bad news, he took it hard; and then he seemed to disappear from the face of the earth. However, the woman, who called herself "the Black" in her ads, did not die, and when she recovered, she did everything she could to find him, but without success.

"I can now tell you the rest of the story. The reason the Lion did not respond is that he has been down in Colombia, living out in the jungle, hunting and exporting wild birds. It wasn't until he happened by chance to see the Black's picture on a magazine cover that he realized what had happened and began his journey back to her.

"Ladies and gentlemen, today, on our flight, we are taking the Lion home to his Black Beauty!"

A cheer went from the passengers, almost drowning out the next announcement.

('To celebrate this grand occasion, Voodoo Charters will be serving champagne on the house!"

Again, a thunderous roar rocked the DC-3 and passengers started to crowd around David. They all wanted to hear his story firsthand. How did he find out the Black was dead? However, did he come to be an exotic bird exporter? Would the Black be waiting for him at the airport? When would they get married?

There was quite a party on that flight. David, who had been hoping to get some rest, instead spent most of his time answering questions and signing autographs. Men shook his hand, women gave him a hug and a kiss. He took it all with good-natured amazement. Evidently, Rachel had really created a stir over his disappearance. He began to realize the depth of her love.

When at last the plane touched down in Seattle, the roar of the in-flight party turned into an excited buzz. The stewardess came down the aisle to David.

"Would you like to get off first? I know the Black must be anxious to see you." Before he could answer, she continued, "Or would you like to be the last one out, so that all these people can enjoy your reunion with you?"

David smiled resignedly. "Of course, I'd be happy to go last."

As the passengers filed out, many of them patted him on the shoulder, saying, "I'm so glad I got to meet you, "Good luck, you deserve it," "Such a romantic story!" Finally, it was David's turn.

The charter plane did not have a regular gate to which it taxied; instead, it had been directed to one at end of Runway Number Three where portable stairs allowed passengers to disembark directly onto the tarmac.

As David came out of the doorway, he expected to see Rachel at the bottom of the stairway waiting for him; instead, he saw people lots of people—lined along the pathway that led toward the terminal.

As he descended into the sea of faces, a roar went up from the crowd. "There he is, it's the Lion," he heard a woman cry. The crowd started to chant "Lion and the Black, Lion and the Black" as David continued through the throng. He was flabbergasted at the reception he was receiving, overwhelmed by the electricity he felt emanating from these people, all strangers who were caught up in the real-life romance of the Lion and the Black.

As he got closer to the building, the pathway curved around and he saw bleachers crammed with spectators, several RIV cameras and a jumble of microphones, and, finally, Rachel.

Rachel — wearing a simple cream-colored satin gown, her black hair cascading in curls down her back, her striking face framed by a halo of baby's breath.

Rachel — whose spirit and determination wouldn't let her give up until they were reunited.

Rachel — his love, his soulmate, his beautiful Black.

He moved forward as if in a dream, shutting out   everyone else but her. He enveloped Rachel in his arms, first locking into the gaze from her warm brown eyes and then sinking into a kiss that seemed to last an eternity. He could feel her eager response, and then suddenly her body went limp as she collapsed in his arms. So intense was the animal magnetism, the raw sexual energy, the ardent emotion between the two lovers that several women in the crowd, caught up in the passion of the moment, fainted on the spot. After several minutes, David broke the embrace and stood back a bit to look into Rachel's eyes.

"My Black Beauty," he said simply.

Rachel locked into his gaze. A bit unsteady at first, she regained her composure and replied in a voice filled with wonder, "1 can't believe you're really here. You don't know what I've been through trying to find you. I just knew you wouldn't desert me, but I had no idea where you'd gone. I thought you were dead — I . . . I was thinking of joining you.

"Hush," David whispered into her hair, "nothing will ever separate us again."

For the first time he noticed people standing nearby, people who were not strangers. One was a man with a kind face, tall and slender. David immediately recognized the short-cropped dark hair with deep ebony eyes.

"Reverend Anderson," said David with genuine delight, reaching out to shake the minister's hand. "How did you get here?"

The reverend laughed. "You're about to marry a very determined woman," he advised. "She tracked me down in Washington, D.C., and said I was the only man who could do the job."

Johnny Anderson had met David when both were stationed on Shimia Island, a little-known outpost in the Aleutian Islands. David had been sent there to trap and relocate the blue foxes that inhabited that desolate piece of real estate. Pastor Anderson's job had been to give spiritual counseling to the nearly 400 soldiers stationed there,
whose assignment was to eavesdrop on any Russian military activity. David and the minister had spent many a long winter's night discussing philosophy and religion.

Next to Reverend Anderson stood Terry and Jill.
"Hey, buddy, am I glad to see you!" said Terry, pumping David's hand. "You had us worried. Why the hell didn't you tell someone where you were going?"

Jill planted a kiss on David's cheek. "I'm so happy for you," she said with a shy smile. "And this is all so exciting! You'd better get used to being a celebrity."
A little behind Jill, David saw another familiar face, that of Dick Sloane. He, too, grabbed David's hand and extended his congratulations. "Quite a story, big guy," he said, giving David a sly wink.

David looked at the three of them in puzzlement.
"How did you get here?" he asked. "You didn't even know Rachel."
Terry laughed his big, booming laugh. "Everybody knows Rachel," he told David, slapping him on the back. "She's been on

TV, in newspapers and magazines — you name it looking for you. Once I read the article in Time, it wasn't hard to track her down. But none of us knew where you were."

"David," said Rachel, grabbing his hand and leading him to an older couple standing next to her. "These are my parents, Walter and Lydia."

Walter, a tall, vigorous man with a firm handshake, looked David over once before saying, "Welcome home, David. It's a pleasure to finally meet you." He paused, seemingly at a loss for words. "You're too old for me to be handing out advice, and I'm not much good at it anyway. I'll just say this: Rachel's been through hell the last few months — I hope you'll make it up to her."

David nodded, wondering what he could say to reassure Walter. Luckily, Lydia made a reply unnecessary.

"Oh, Walter, for goodness' sake! Give the young man a chance." She put her arms around David and gave him an affectionate squeeze. "We're so happy for both of you, dear. I just know you and Rachel will have a wonderful life together."

"Believe me, I will do everything in my power to make sure we do," he replied, returning her hug.

David moved back to Rachel's side and again took her in his arms.

"Are you ready?" he asked.

Rachel nodded.

Terry took his place next to David, thrusting a small box in his hand which contained a simple wedding band. The Reverend Anderson stood in front of the couple and recited the words which would join them together forever. When he reached the culmination of the short ceremony and said, "David, you may now kiss the bride," the mob erupted again. David and Rachel once again came together in a long, sensuous, crowd-pleasing embrace which had women swooning into the arms of strangers.

The media, which had been contained by security guards until the ceremony was over, were finally let loose to descend upon the couple. David and Rachel found themselves surrounded by microphones and cameras, blinking at the bright lights as they tried to answer questions.

"How does it feel to be home?"

"What were you doing in Colombia?" "How did you finally find each other?"

"Is the Black as beautiful as you remember?"

"How much money did you spend to find the Lion?"

David and Rachel answered as many questions as they could before being ushered to the electric tram that serviced the northern satellite of the terminal.

"Where are we going?" asked David.

"You'll see."

As the wedding party jumped on board, many of the well-wishers crammed in with them while others were left to wait for the next train. After a short trip, the tram doors opened to the large open space of the satellite terminal, where several hundred more people awaited the Lion and the Black. As the couple exited the train, the crowd, which had been waiting expectantly, started to cheer and to chant: "Lion and the Black, Lion and the Black."

Rachel beamed and waved; David stared in amazement. He was stunned by the reception, "My, God! What have you created?" he whispered into Rachel's ear.

The whole south end of the terminal had been beautifully decorated, complete with hundreds of roses of all colors, a champagne fountain, and a huge wedding cake. As Rachel and David made their way through the crowd, an attractive man strode toward them, extending his hand.

"David, Rachel, I'm so pleased to meet you. I'm Mayor Halsey." He smiled warmly at them, then turned to the crowd. "Ladies and gentlemen, the Pacific Northwest has its very own love story to rival that of Romeo and Juliet. What's more, this one ends much more happily. May I present to you the Lion and the Black." The crowd roared its approval and the mayor turned back to the couple. "Your story has touched the hearts of thousands of people, both here in Seattle and across the country, and it has inspired one man to create something very special. He'd like to present it to you as a wedding gift."

The mayor motioned for a diminutive man standing off to the side to come forward. He approached David and Rachel nervously, standing in front of them tongue-tied until the mayor came to his rescue.

"This is Mr. Kahn, a jeweler here in town. He has designed, and made by hand, a medallion to commemorate this special occasion."
On cue, Mr. Kahn opened the small black-velvet jewelry box and presented it to Rachel. Inside lay a gold medallion attached to a fine gold chain.

"Oh, it's lovely!" exclaimed Rachel, as she picked it up to examine it. Pictured on one side was the profile of woman with fine features and long, straight hair cascading down past her shoulders. The inscription below it read "THE BLACK." The flip side featured the head of a lion in full roar; inscribed beneath this picture were the words "THE LION." The woman's hair and the lion's mane were made of inlaid onyx, providing dramatic contrast to the gold.

"Mr. Kahn, it's exquisite, but I'm afraid we couldn't accept this!" protested Rachel, closing the box and handing it back to the jeweler. "It's much too valuable a piece.

The little man spoke for the first time. "No, please," he insisted. "I want you to have it, and one for the Lion, too, if he would like. Please don't worry about the cost. I plan to make many more, and I'm sure I will be well compensated for my efforts."

Overwhelmed, the couple accepted graciously, giving the man their sincere thanks for such a unique and precious gift. Then David led Rachel to a table where a bottle of Dom Perignon and two crystal goblets awaited them. After carefully filling their glasses, he handed one to Rachel. "I think this might be the right time to offer a toast to my bride." He lifted his glass and smiled at Rachel. "To the woman whose beauty radiates from the inside out — to Rachel, my exquisite Black." He bent to kiss her softly, and their guests clapped and cheered. "And now, everyone, join us in celebrating our new life together."

David and Rachel spent the next two hours reveling in the merrymaking with friends and strangers alike. They held hands continually, and each time they kissed, someone in the crowd would faint from the sheer intensity of their passion. Finally, Rachel motioned that it was time to go, and the well-wishers escorted them to the tram, showering them with flower petals along the way. Upon reaching the main terminal, Rachel led David out to a waiting limousine. Night had long since fallen and a nearly full moon shone down on them.

"Good evening," said the driver as he opened the door for the couple.

"Now what?" asked David. "I hope we're going home. I just want to be alone with you, to hold you in my arms, and make up for all the time we've been apart."

"Soon, my Lion," said Rachel. She nestled back into David's arms and signaled to the driver. As the car moved forward, David noticed two motorcycle policemen acting as escorts.

"Are they with us?" he asked.

"I think so," said Rachel.

David shook his head in amazement. "Are we so famous that we can't go anywhere without a police escort?"

Rachel laughed. "Only for a little while. It'll die down.

The limousine headed into traffic, driving north toward the city, which offered a shimmering view of lighted skyscrapers silhouetted against the dark sky and distant ferries moving to and from across the sound.

Twenty minutes later, the limousine pulled up to the famed Edgewater Hotel. When they got out, Rachel didn't bother to stop at the reception desk but headed straight for the elevators where she pressed "P" for penthouse. Up, up, up they traveled to the top story, where, when the doors opened, they were greeted by the most luxurious accommodations David had ever seen.

"Wow!" he exclaimed, looking first around the apartment, and then out at the harbor dotted with the lights of seagoing craft. "This is spectacular!" He put his arms around Rachel and whispered, "You are spectacular. You are better than I remembered, more than I had ever hoped for. I am the luckiest man in the world."

He kissed her deeply and pulled her down onto the king-sized bed, where they spent the next two days together.

Back at Rachel's house, the light on her answering machine blinked insistently. The message awaiting David and Rachel was one that would change their lives forever.